HE

A remarkable tale of romance and resilience

Larry Benjamin

Beaten Track
www.beatentrackpublishing.com

He

First published 2025 by Beaten Track Publishing
Copyright © 2025 Larry Benjamin

Print ISBN: 978 1 78645 675 5
eBook ISBN: 978 1 78645 676 2

Beaten Track Publishing,
Burscough, Lancashire.
www.beatentrackpublishing.com

Parce que c'était lui; parce que c'était moi

—*Michel de Montaigne*

Every lover's got a little dagger in their hand.

—*Fall Out Boy*

CONTENTS

In memory of Mark Stephen Johnson
August 24, 1957 – March 28, 2024
There is you in everything I do.

And for Deb McGowan who's been my publisher and editor,
friend and fiercest supporter for a decade. I wish this writer
had the words to express his gratitude for you.

PROLOGUE

Oren Strange walked into *Abattoir* and sniffed the air. The former slaughterhouse may have been renamed and refurbished, but it still stank of violence and agony and blood. Sawdust, which covered the floor, swirled about his feet as he took reluctant steps forward. Paper streamers, purple and white—his school colors—hanging from the low ceiling, tickling his shoulders, felt like ghosts brushing past.

Why was he here, he wondered again. Because of Rio, of course. He'd confessed his secret, and its release had unexpectedly opened a door he hadn't known he'd held the key to. Now that he was here, all he had to do was walk through it. The question was, could he? If he hadn't told Rio his secret, Rio would never have asked him to come. What more, Oren wondered, did Rio want from him? Why was he so eager to see him after all these years?

Had his life not recently fallen, unexpectedly, apart, he wouldn't have found himself here at this reunion, ready to step through that newly opened door. Oren walked up to a table just beyond the entrance where plastic-encased name tags rested in alphabetical order.

"O Strange One," a voice suddenly boomed as Oren studied the display looking for his name. The old hated moniker that so many had thought such a clever play on his name. The voice was attached to the dense heavy body of a former athlete who had let himself go to seed, surrendering to age, gravity, and too much

1

beer; the muscle had dissolved into fat and settled around his middle. Lidell Holloway.

"You look exactly the same," Lidell boomed. "Still skinny as a rail."

"I'm sorry," Oren said. "Do I know you?"

Immediately, the bravado left Lidell and was replaced by a kind of bitterness, for Oren had reminded him that he was no longer the star athlete, wasn't otherwise anyone worth remembering. Lidell abruptly slunk away muttering to himself. His voice was so low, but Oren heard what he said: "Stuck up, citified faggot." *So, nothing has changed*, Oren thought to himself.

After their exchange, doubt assailed Oren once again and arrested his progress. He stood still trying to adjust to the room's heat, the cigarette smoke, the cloying scent of White Diamonds. Why was he here? Was he, like Jackson, just trying to rewrite his story with a different leading man and a happier ending?

Then, from the center of a gaggle of twittering, giggling women wearing their Sunday best and "good" bras, gold crosses hanging around chicken necks plunging and twisting between pushed-up bosoms like the agony of Christ, he heard a rumble of laughter; like echoes of thunder up at the quarry, it went on and on. It was the most absurd sound in the world, a laugh he recognized. Rio was here, as he'd promised he would be. Whatever else had changed about Rio, his laugh was the same. Oren found that reassuring. Now the only remaining question was, did he have the courage to step through that open door that invited like a portal into another dimension?

Oren took his name tag off the table and shoved it in his pocket.

BOOK ONE:
1975–1981

RED (1975)

Monday, January 6, 1975, Locust Hollow—His name is Rio. He has creamy brown skin, and his small shapely head is crowned with loose unruly curls that refuse to be tamed by cut or comb; his eyes are the color of the smoke from a California wildfire. He's slim but broad-shouldered; he's lean and angular, sharp as the blade of a new knife. Having been born in Mexico, English is not his first language; he has the faintest accent. He is musical, but there is something of the poet in him, too. He seems always to be laughing. Like erupting lava, his laughter flows easily, encompassing everything in its path. Looking at him—and I can't seem to stop looking at him—I understand myself for the first time; I want to be him.

Since I can remember, I've admired and envied my classmates, boys who were handsome, muscular, athletic, manly despite their childish ways, even as I preferred kneading dough in a warm kitchen or scrubbing copper pots until they shone to hacking through ice to capture fish comatose from the cold or wringing the necks of defenseless chickens too dumb to close their mouths during a rainstorm.

I spent all of freshman year and last term wanting to be like Rio, to look like him, to speak with his deep voice, to attract friends and teachers' praise. To have his confidence. He is so at ease with the knowledge that he is good-looking that he seems the slightest bit cocky, which doesn't detract at all from his allure. Rio. I'd thought I simply wanted to look like this handsome boy

I admired, *be* him; I wanted to be strong and handsome and manly. It wasn't until I saw Rio, who was wearing a tight red polo shirt in homeroom this morning—he was in Mexico over Christmas break, so he is darker, and he seems to have gotten handsomer and more muscular while he was away—that I realized I don't want to *be* him so much as I want to be *with* him. It was, I realized suddenly, that simple and that profound. I want to touch him, to feel his hands around my waist. I want to feel his warm breath on my neck. I want to press my lips against his, to hold his hand as we walk down a deserted country road. I want to swim naked with him up at the quarry.

With this sudden clarity, I now understand why I would rush home from school to catch the four-thirty movie whenever it was Elvis Presley Week. I hadn't understood why I loved watching him, with his slicked-back pompadour, his long body sheathed in tight shirts and form-fitting pants, and the sound of his voice. Mesmerized, I'd watched his movies: *Viva Las Vegas*; *Jailhouse Rock*; *King Creole*; *Blue Suede Shoes*; *Blue Hawaii*. Later, I'd been equally enthralled by David Cassidy in *The Partridge Family*, with his flowing protein-enriched hair and his skintight bellbottoms.

Monday, April 14, 1975, Locust Hollow—I had my first wet dream last night. Not surprisingly, it was about Rio. Much of it wasn't clear, but he held me tightly against him with a viselike grip. I couldn't get away, but I didn't want to either; instead, I was content with the rubbing together of our bodies, his breath mingling with mine.

They told us about wet dreams, calling them "nocturnal emissions" in sex-ed class, but our teacher made them sound akin to wetting the bed and thus shameful for a teenager to fall prey to. The viscous stickiness was nothing like pee and its expulsion was far more pleasurable than the simple act of pissing. I didn't go to school today, claiming to be sick. I've spent most of the day lying in bed, with my eyes closed and breathing deeply, trying to bring on another dream. So far, no luck.

Tuesday, June 24, 1975, Locust Hollow—The evening was failing, light slipping from the sky. I lay on my bed, my arms behind my head, and luxuriated in the feeling of having nothing to do. School was over and I had no chores to do, which is unusual. Reverend Jack is fond of declaring idle hands are the devil's workshop, so my grandfather endeavors to keep these hands of mine busy. And on the farm, something always needs doing: animals need to be fed; shit needs to be raked; something needs to be plucked out of the ground, striated with dirt and fertilizer. Though my brothers, under Grandfather's tutelage, only seem to engage in play and mischief and the violence of pigeon shooting.

My hands and my mind, free to wander, inevitably—for he filled every corner of my mind—drifted to images of Rio. Rio, shirtless in boxer shorts in the locker room, a thin coat of sweat like mineral oil clinging to his shoulders and chest. It's hot in my room at the top of the house; we don't have air conditioning. The two window fans in my bedroom window do nothing to cool the air because my grandfather insists on putting them in the windows backwards so they can "draw the hot air out."

No one in Locust Hollow has air conditioning—even window units are too expensive—except Reverend Jack, who has it in his house and in his office at the church, though the church itself, where we sweat all spring and summer as if sweat could purge sin like tears can release grief, remains without air conditioning. But no one in the congregation seems to mind because they think Reverend Jack needs to be comfortable and cool to craft his fiery inspirational sermons—grounded in fire and brimstone and hell's heat—that guide his flock.

My hand drifted to my dick. After, I tossed the sock under my bed with the one from yesterday, and the one from the day before, and the day before *that*, feeling guilty as if I'd stolen something from Rio when he wasn't looking. I drifted into sleep, swearing I would stop doing this. Maybe I would start joining my brothers and our grandfather in their relentless shooting of pigeons, strangling of chickens, and tossing around a football in the dust—all of which they did with seeming joy and all for reasons I simply cannot fathom.

Sunday, July 1975, Locust Hollow—Locust Hollow, where we live—if you can call my existence in this hopeless place after my parents uprooted us from Springfield, living—where the farm is above all a story of failure and loss. Throughout the Hollow's history, industry has swept in, like a plague of locusts, consuming its resources, then abandoning its fleshless carcass, leaving rusty bones to bleach and decay in the sun. First there were the stone quarries dug out of the hills that surrounded the town, depleted their treasures, then abandoned them. Then came the steel mills, now shuttered and rusting. There's still a blouse and shirt factory in the next town, though. That's where most people in Locust Hollow work.

I work three afternoons and Saturday mornings at Lewisohn's, the lone department store in town—a family-owned emporium that sells "seconds" and last season's fashions at discounted prices. Even the rarefied imported chocolates are discounted, as they are typically nearing their "best by" date. I'm spared working Sundays because Locust Hollow still has blue laws on the books so no business is open after six p.m. on Wednesdays or on Sundays, so the populace, in need of saving, can attend Wednesday evening Bible study and spend all day Sunday in church repenting their sins and praying for others too firmly in the devil's grasp to come to church to pray for themselves.

Mostly, I work so I can save for college and get the hell out of this godforsaken town—but also to escape my grandfather's ill will, my brothers' savagery, and the general gloom of the farm. It hasn't always been like this; I haven't always been discontented. Everything changed the summer after my grandmother died. I remember her as a rotund woman with graying hair. In my mind's eye, I see her moving about the kitchen with purpose, covered in flour and speckled with blood.

After we moved to the farm following Grandma's death, my world grew slowly dimmer, darkening until I found myself at midnight on the crest of a great crater, stumbling from place to place, foothold to foothold. My mother got pregnant in rapid succession and gave birth to my brothers. There followed the smell of alcohol and shouted words. Grief and violence blew past me like tumbleweed.

Friday, August 15, 1975, Locust Hollow—Every August, the migrant fruit workers arrive to pick pears, switching to apples in the early fall. By the end of October, they are gone.

To earn extra money, I join in the fruit picking in August, picking in the afternoons and Sundays once school starts, gathering pears and apples beside the migrant workers until the end of October.

It is a gypsy's life, itinerant, drifting from farm to farm, state to state, following the picking season like a carelessly drawn map. The migrant workers' stories, when I can bridge the language barrier, are fascinating. Theirs is a hard life, grounded in insecurity and often cruelty. So not much different to my own. There is a kind of freedom and hope in their lives I can't help envying. Perhaps with a change in landscape, their situation would improve. At any rate, within weeks, the people around them, their *landscape* would change; mine never does.

Every year since I turned fourteen, I've joined in the fruit picking. Near the end of each summer, which is when picking season starts, hope would be conceived within me. By the end of picking season, which coincides with the start of midterms, hope, nurtured, prayed for, would be stillborn, brown, crumbled, trampled underfoot, and left to blow in the fall winds as carelessly as the falling leaves.

This year felt different, though—I could feel it from the beginning. And I was sure this year would be different; the child, hope, would be carried to term this time and grow and thrive.

Usually, the same workers return year after year, and you begin to recognize them. Sometimes, though, there are new faces. This year, one of the new workers, a guy a little older than I named Juan, really stands out. He's good-looking and broad-shouldered with an easy manner and a tumult of dark hair. He picks more fruit than anyone. I like watching him as his muscles shift beneath his bronze skin with his quick, efficient movements.

I was standing near the converted school bus that sells cuchifritos, a variety of Puerto Rican foods that are usually pork based and fried. The bus is only open during picking season and is quite popular with the migrant workers. They serve blood sausage, fried potato balls stuffed with meat, fried pork skin, and plantains. They sell juices that seem exotic to me: passionfruit, pineapple, coconut.

I was lingering near the bus this afternoon, waiting for the line to thin so I could discreetly examine the offerings at the shabby newsstand next to the bus, which was also only open during picking season and which sold Spanish language newspapers and magazines and *Playboy* and a magazine called *Blueboy*, in whose pages last summer I'd seen my first naked man. In the picture, he was wearing a polo shirt with horizontal stripes, chest hair peeking out of the shirt's unbuttoned collar and...nothing else. I'd been mesmerized but too frightened to buy it and too scared to steal it. Ever since, I've wondered if that is what Rio looks like under his clothes; I wonder if I'll ever find out.

Suddenly addressing me, without turning around, Juan said, "Take a picture. It'll last longer."

"Excuse me?" I said, stepping back. Had he seen me edging towards the magazine rack?

He turned around. "I said take a picture—it'll last longer."

"Huh?" I said, staring at him. I'd never been this close to him before. He was even handsomer than he looked at a distance.

"You're always staring at me—"

"I—I—I'm not—" I was lying, and we both knew it. This close, I thought he might be handsomer than Rio.

He looked around, lowered his voice. "I know what you are, what you want."

"I—"

"See the thing is, I don't mind." He watched me closely then said, "Follow me." He led me deep into the orchard where all the fruit had already been picked. Leaning against a tree, he unbuckled his jeans and pushed them to his knees; to my shock, he wore no underwear. "C'mon," he said roughly. "Have at it before someone comes along."

I dropped to my knees as if I knew what I was doing.

In the act, in his touch, there had been tenderness, an occasional caress. After he tucked himself away and zipped up his pants, I stood and asked, "Can I kiss you?"

He looked startled, then displeased, then offered me his mouth. After a few tentative pecks, his lips parted, and his tongue began to explore my mouth. He relaxed and, sucking on my tongue, lapped up the taste of himself. I barely registered the narcissism of those first kisses. When we broke apart, he shoved me away from him so hard I stumbled and almost fell. Tears sprang to my eyes.

"Don't," he growled, "come near me again. You hear me? If you do, I'll break your neck. In fact, don't even look at me." He turned and walked away.

As hurt and confused as I was by his sudden change in mood, kissing him had solved the riddle of me, finally. With that single kiss, I learned definitively who I am and what I want. The question now is, what do I do with this knowledge?

Saturday, September 13, 1975, Locust Hollow—As I've continued on with picking, I've been doing my best to stay as far away from Juan as possible, partly because the whole thing was kind of humiliating and also because I'm tired of getting hit. So, I was surprised when I was leaving my shift today and spotted him smoking a cigarette at the orchard entrance. I turned to head back into the thicket of trees to wait until he left.

"Hey! Wait up," he called.

I froze. When he reached me, he reached out and squeezed my shoulder. I flinched. He withdrew his hand. "Hey, man. Sorry about the other day. I didn't mean what I said. I never did anything with a guy before. I just freaked out a little. It kind of scared me how much I liked what we did." When I said nothing, he continued, "C'mon. Let me make it up to you?"

"How?" I asked.

"Let's go back to our spot and I'll let you suck me off again. I'll even let you kiss me if you want." He grinned. This time, when it was over, *he* kissed *me* and caressed my neck.

Saturday, October 11, 1975, Locust Hollow—I turned sixteen today. My grandfather didn't remember my birthday was today. Or maybe he felt it wasn't worth mentioning. After he found religion, after my parents died, he's come to believe that unless you are Jesus Christ, you shouldn't expect a fuss on your birthday. In all fairness, I don't know when his birthday is, either.

In Springfield, with Grampy Eddie, my birthday meant visits to the zoo and the toy department at Woolworth's and once a trip to the circus. But as he liked to point out, Grampy Eddie was a fan of "the grand gesture." This meant two dozen yellows roses for Mommy on Mother's Day and the tallest, fattest Christmas tree in Springfield each year, under which he'd place stacks of gaily wrapped gifts of every description.

I've pretty much resigned myself to the notion that my birthday is just another day, no more worthy of recognition than any other Tuesday or Wednesday. So, I was surprised when at the end of picking, as it was growing dark, Juan wished me happy birthday. Grasping my wrist, he pulled me back into the orchard. Stopping, he pulled us to the ground against a tree. When I looked at him quizzically, he said, "A lot of girls want me. You're a cute guy. I bet a lot of girls want you, too. But you only want me." He actually sounded proud. "I think that's so hot. Being with you makes me feel more like a man because girls want you, but I'm such a man, *you* want *me*."

I was confused by what he was saying. For one thing, I couldn't imagine any girls being interested in me. I certainly wasn't interested in them. But he was right—I did want him. When I reached for his belt, he pushed me back against the tree.

"Relax," he said. "I'm leaving the day after tomorrow, and today is your birthday. Let me do it."

Before I could ask what it was he wanted me to let him do, he'd unbuttoned my shirt and pulled one of my nipples into his mouth while pinching the other between his thumb and forefinger. I thought for a minute I might pass out from the mix of pain and pleasure. Next, he undid my belt and tugged down my dungarees and jockey shorts. Almost before I realized where this was heading, he had me in his mouth doing to me what I'd spent most of that picking season doing to him.

He pulled away abruptly. "Don't," he admonished, "come in my mouth."

I nodded weakly, astonished and confused. How had we come to change places? My hands found their way into his tumultuous hair; I'd never left anything so luxurious, except maybe his mouth enveloping me...

"Stop," I shouted pushing him away. He rocked back on the balls of his feet as my come shot onto my chest and shoulder and chin.

"Holy crap," he said. "Don't ever fuck a woman. You'll get her pregnant for sure!"

Happy sixteenth birthday to me.

Sunday, November 23, 1975, Locust Hollow—In church today, Reverend Jack told us as our Thanksgiving Fellowship dinner is fast approaching, we should reflect on what we are most grateful for. I think I'm most grateful for Juan, who I miss. Though, of course, I cannot say this out loud to anyone, let alone at the Fellowship dinner table.

If Rio first introduced me to myself, it was Juan who confirmed my suspicions and expanded my world view; it isn't just Rio I want but a boy in general. I'd thought my love, my *lust* for Rio was unique and special and limited to just he and I. I thought Michel de Montaigne, one of the most significant philosophers of the French Renaissance, had expressed my and Rio's situation perfectly; when asked why he loved his deceased friend Etienne de La Boétie so much, he'd simply replied, "Parce que c'était lui; parce que c'était moi"—*Because it was he; because it was I.* It turns out to be something more diffuse, a more generalized proclivity. Something I don't even have a word for.

But whereas with Rio, I dream of a future, a life together, my relationship with Juan, brief as it was, seemed temporary, transactional, and once he got off, the brief exchange of affection, if not altogether forgotten, was diminished, pushed aside, a youthful indulgence driven by hormones and accessibility.

Perhaps because I'm only sixteen, or maybe just because I'm so lonely, I've attached too much romantic significance to my encounters with Juan, for if there's sex and a bit of affection in his touch, it must be love, right?

I wonder if it would be different with Rio.

ORANGE (1976)

Friday, March 26, 1976, Locust Hollow—I was sitting in the bleachers in the gym watching Rio and the other boys play basketball. I'm a bad player—disinterested in the sport, not competitive—so no one ever wants me on their team. Mr. Gold usually excuses me and sends me to sit in the bleachers. I'm always there alone, so I was surprised when he walked up and slid across the bench until he was a couple of feet from me—not so close that he'd have to scamper away if I rejected his advance but not so far that he had to shout.

"Can I ask you a question?"

Sure," I said. No one really talks to me, so I was curious.

"Why are you always staring at Rio? What do you see in him?"

"He's so...handsome." Realizing I'd probably said the wrong thing, I quickly added, "I wish I looked like him." I knew that wasn't true. It was more than that. It was simpler than that, but it was also more than I could tell this strange boy.

"Yeah, he is. And he has a great body. But he knows it. It makes him arrogant. But you're really cute..."

"Me?" I asked, literally pointing at my freckled, speckled self and my jug-handle ears.

"Yeah, you. You're cute, but you don't seem to know it. And you're sweet and kind, even though people aren't kind to you. That, to me,

17

makes you far more handsome than Rio, so I don't know why you'd wish to look like him."

When I said nothing, he seemed to grow exasperated. "Look," he said, "you've clearly not noticed, being so obsessed with Rio and all, but I've liked you since sophomore year." Still, I said nothing, and he continued in a rush, "I mean I like you—like I'm supposed to like girls."

His words made me feel unmoored, light-headed. *This is what it must feel like to be intoxicated*, I thought. How had my parents stood it?

When I still said nothing, he hesitated, then, less sure, continued, "You like guys, right?"

I thought of Rio, how that day last January, he walked into our homeroom and changed everything. I thought of Juan, the only boy I'd ever kissed and had sex with. I've been bereft and alone ever since he left, but he left me entirely sure of who and *what* I am.

"Yes," I answered.

"Would you like to hang out sometime?"

"Hang out?" I repeated stupidly.

"Yeah," he said. "Like go on a date. We could go on a picnic or maybe go swimming in the quarry. I just want to hang out with you. OK?"

I recognized him, of course. His name is Jackson. He is Reverend Jack's son. "My name is Jackson," he always says whenever some new person calls him Jack. "Jackson, not Jack. Jack is my father. Please don't ever call me Jack." I know him from school and from church, where people are always praying over us, which feels like bludgeoning, the New Testament their cudgel. I hadn't understood why until Rio. These prayers are led by Reverend Jack, who is like a Nordic wind: cold, relentless. His voice, though, is all heat: hellfire and damnation. Even his comfort, offered grudgingly to his flock and under extreme duress and filled with resentment, is cold. There is no shelter in his Bible. Reverend Jack is terrifying.

I looked at Jackson more closely. We are roughly the same height and build, but where he is muscular, I am slender. I look like my mother; if she had been a boy, she would have looked like me. He gives off a heady masculinity that is absent from me. I find it enticing, dizzy making, like smelling strong perfume or drinking pop too fast. His eyes are melancholy, his mood blue. He is square jawed; even at just seventeen, his face is craggy, pitted with the memory of pubescent acne. He looks like he was hacked from flint. Jackson looks like a thug, but there is nothing of the thug in his manner or demeanor. He's handsome. I'm not, even if he says I am. His manner is as rough as his hands. I tried to remember what I know about him.

The other kids dislike him, freeze him out. If I am outside their circle, Jackson is on the moon. They say it's "cuz he ain't like us." Him asking me out on a date made me realize that he isn't like them, and neither am I, but now I understand he is like me. They say he can't be trusted because he is a PK, a preacher's kid, and assumed to be a "narc," spying for Christ, reporting, judging. And maybe that's why Jackson likes me, sought me out—because he is different, as different as I am.

If I'm honest with myself, I have to admit I've noticed Jackson before. He is one of those masculine boys I admire. He can catch a baseball and dribble a basketball; he's good at shop class, whether it's building a birdhouse or a transistor radio or a small motor. He's helped me a few times when I've struggled to complete whatever project we are assigned. He is singularly attractive in some indefinable but concrete way—but even in my lonely state, it hadn't seemed wise to spend too much time lusting over the son of Reverend Fire-and-Brimstone.

"So do you want to go out with me or not?" he asked, pulling me from my thoughts.

I remembered my first time with a boy—my *only* time, actually. It had been awkward and hurried. After, he'd seemed embarrassed, though when I asked if I could kiss him, Juan said yes. That kiss, more than the sex, is what convinced me, solidified the knowledge of who I am, that this was what I wanted. What I did not want was secrecy, to be forced to skulk about like a criminal, clinging to the shadows, unable to make or endure eye contact. Rio and I, I had decided, would love in the light.

Now here was this boy, a boy like me who liked me, offering to pull me into the light.

"Yes," I said.

Saturday, April 3, 1976, Locust Hollow—Today, Jackson and I went on our first date. He drove me in his old bright-orange pickup truck up to the orchard for a picnic. His mother had packed him a wonderful lunch, no doubt expecting he was going to take some girl a-courting.

"Can I ask you a question?"

"Sure," I said, biting into a slice of watermelon; its juice ran down my chin. Jackson wiped the trailing juice away with his finger and placed his finger in his mouth, sucking off the juice. I was instantly aroused.

"Why would you," he began, withdrawing his finger from his mouth, "like Rio? I mean, why would you like a boy who doesn't like other boys?"

"I didn't know there were other boys who liked other boys. I thought I was the only one." Normally, I would have been embarrassed to admit something so naïve, but already with Jackson, I felt safe and able to express any thought I had. "I thought Rio might end up liking me because I am me, as I like him because he is he."

Jackson cocked his head to the side and pulled a slice of watermelon out of an iced plastic bag. "You're a strange bird," he said. "You don't think like—or even talk like, for that matter—anyone I've ever known, but I'm glad you like boys because I *really like you*."

I was getting warm, so I pulled my long-sleeved polo over my head. Noticing the series of tiny spots lighter than the rest of me and red in some places along my arms and around the fingers of my left hand, Jackson asked, "Do you have a rash?"

"Sort of," I said, feeling suddenly self-conscious. "I have eczema. It's on my legs too."

"Does it hurt?" he asked, looking concerned.

"No, not really. It's uncomfortable, and sometimes it gets really itchy." I did not tell him that when I was younger, I used to run my hand and my arms under the hot water faucet in the bathroom, preferring the feeling of being burned to the ceaseless itching. I did not tell him the worst part of it had been the constant teasing, the echoing taunts...*icky skin, icky skin*...and my grandfather's insistence, "There ain't nothin' wrong with you, boy. It's all in your head."

"Is there anything you can do for it?"

"Yeah, I use a steroidal cream when it flares up and Lubriderm lotion, which the apothecary orders special for me. I lotion…*a lot*. That helps. Doctor says I'll outgrow it." Which I found ridiculous because he made a skin condition sound like the pair of high-top white shoes a toddler might wear. Still feeling self-conscious, I reached for my polo shirt again.

"You don't have to cover up from me," Jackson said softly. He cocked his head. "Is that why you're so shy? You know, it's not so bad to look at, and besides, it makes you, you."

I closed my eyes and tried to let his words wash away the years of misery, the teasing.

We talked of other things after that—I don't remember what. But I remember never having felt so at ease with someone before.

Saturday, May 1, 1976, Locust Hollow—It's been a month since Jackson told me he liked me. We've become friends. I definitely like him back. When I'm with him, I have a sense of contentment that I haven't felt since we moved to the farm. So, I was disappointed today when he told me we couldn't meet up because his father wanted him to plant a garden in front of the church. I couldn't imagine this because the ground in front of the church is all concrete slabs, hot as hell in the summer and slippery as an iceberg in winter. Curious, wanting to see him, I hopped on my bike and rode to the church.

The road was rutted, dry, and cracked and kicked up so much dust I ended up walking the bike mostly. I saw Jackson, shirtless in the midday sun, covered in sweat and slamming a pickaxe against the unyielding ground. I'd never seen him shirtless before. He was much more muscular than I would have imagined. Black hair curled out from under his arms and across his chest; his nipples rose like succulents from the wild grasses of his dark chest hair. Farther down, where his hair thinned into a narrow trail leading to his waist, the mound of his protuberant navel, like a scoop of ice cream or a sand dune on his flat stomach, peeked through his hair. Under the worn dungarees he wore, I could just make out the curve of his penis, more prominent and bigger than my own. A surge of desire for him rose up so suddenly and strongly, I thought I might swoon. Steeling myself, moving my bike into position to hide my erection, I called to him, looking just above his head so as not to stare at his nipples or what lay just below his waist.

It seemed to me Reverend Jack had sentenced him to hard labor for some imagined sin, most likely related to me. I mean, who plants a garden in concrete in October? I said as much as I called to him. Jackson shrugged, dropping the pickaxe. "If that's the price of being with you, I'm fine with it," he said. He smiled. That smile warmed me more than the midday sun.

I wasn't strong enough to help him break up the concrete and he only had one pickaxe anyway, so I retrieved the pieces he broke, put them in the wheelbarrow, and dumped them in the weed-choked lot next to the church. As we worked, we talked, sharing our histories easily, eager to learn about each other. Sometimes we fell into a companionable silence.

We spent most of the time talking, though—about everything and nothing. I felt as if the more we learned about each other, the deeper in love we fell, quite as if Cupid, sitting in the trees above us, was, hourly, shooting arrows into the hearts of my sweet young would-be lover and me. It was a heady feeling, and for the first time, I felt the sting of my parents' absence, my loneliness, and the weight of my grandfather's enmity begin to ease.

The sun began its descent, though being so close to Jackson, I felt no cooler.

"We both need to get home to dinner," he said, throwing down his pickaxe and shaking out his corded muscles. He pulled on his T-shirt, and to my disappointment, his succulent nipples and swollen navel disappeared. Growing up, I'd had crushes on, and wet dreams about, Robert Conrad from *The Wild Wild West* and later on Greg Morris from *Mission Impossible*, and of course Rio. But this, *Jackson*, was something else entirely.

Sunday, May 23, 1976, Locust Hollow—Being too old for Sunday children's Bible study, and while the young ones' indoctrination fully occupies his parents' attention, Jackson and I have gotten used to being free to spend time together after service. Usually, we go out to the quarry or poke about the ruins of downtown or go to the old Bijou theatre in the next county where they show old movies all day Sunday for a one-dollar admission fee.

Today, though, we went to his house after service. Once we arrived, he invited me to see his room. I was really nervous. This seems silly to write, but it's true: I was nervous. I'd never been in a boy's bedroom before. Anyway, his room is surprisingly neat and organized. He has a little desk and even the papers on it are in neat stacks and neatly labelled. I looked around curiously and was surprised to see he had a number of clocks, none of which seemed to be working. "What's with the clocks?" I asked, mostly to cover my nervousness but also out of curiosity.

"I collect them," he said.

"I can see that," I said, trying not to smile. "I meant *why do you collect them?*"

"Oh!" He sat, straddling his desk chair backwards. "People always think about their lives in these huge chunks—days, weeks, years. But really, life is made up of moments, of minutes that change your life. I use the clocks to mark and remember those important minutes." He paused. "Now that I've said it out loud, it sounds so dumb—"

"No, it doesn't. I get it. I collect my special moments in a journal."

He looked unconvinced.

"So, each of these clocks is a memory?" I asked.

"Yes."

"What's that one?" I asked, pointing to a yellow Bakelite clock.

He smiled. "That was the first time I had a wet dream—and realized I was becoming a man."

I didn't ask for details, for if he was like me—and he was—I knew what the dream entailed.

"So, what about that one?" I asked, this time pointing to a small square onyx one with a white enamel face and Roman numerals.

"That's when I realized my father's preaching was bullshit."

"So, the preacher's kid doesn't believe?"

"Not in the Church or the Bible or my father's words, no. Do you?"

"No. All that talk of heaven and hell and fire and damnation is annoying as heck. And it's just theatrics."

"You really think so? You don't think there is a heaven and hell?"

I shook my head. "Mr. Lewisohn down at the store is Jewish. He told me once Jews don't believe in heaven and hell. So, I asked him how they made people do the right thing."

"What'd he say?"

"He said the whole point of Judaism was that it taught you to do the right thing, the moral thing, simply because it was the *right* thing, the *moral* thing to do."

He nodded slowly.

I changed the subject. "And that clock?" I asked. This one was a stepped alabaster clock, like a small monument.

"That one marks the first time I noticed you."

"When was that?"

He closed his eyes. "It was sophomore year. We had gym. We were playing softball. As usual, you were chosen last and put in the outfield where you couldn't do any damage. I'll never forget, you were sitting on this big rock reading. Anyway, this guy hit the ball and sent it flying towards the outfield. Everyone was yelling at you to catch the ball—you didn't even have a glove. You looked up at all the screaming and then went back to reading your book as the ball landed behind you. It was so clear you didn't give a crap."

I laughed. "I didn't. Still don't."

"Anyway, it ended up being a homerun for the other team and Lidell, our team's captain, was pissed. He walked up to you and shoved you off the rock. You fell, of course, and he was leaning over you yelling. Instead of getting up, you raised your foot and kicked him square in the balls. He doubled over on the ground holding his junk. You picked up your book, got back on your rock, glanced at him as if you'd just taken out the trash, and went back to reading. Everyone was laughing and screaming."

I smiled, remembering the incident. "I remember that day. I *hate* gym. And Lidell."

Jackson nodded, then, gesturing at his clocks, said, "Do you think I'm pathetic?"

"Because you collect clocks?" When he nodded, I said, "It's not pathetic. I told you I keep a journal so I remember the important moments in my life. It's the same thing as collecting clocks, really."

"Have you written about me in your journal?" he asked.

He looked so hopeful I wanted to cry. "I have," I said.

He nodded, seemingly satisfied but didn't ask if he could read my entries; he grew in my estimation.

"Did you know you liked me then?" I asked him.

"No. But I knew you were special, different. I wanted to get to know you."

He came over and sat on his bed next to me. He took my hand, and rubbing my fingers, he asked, "That's OK, right? That I want to get to know you? That I *like* you?"

"Yeah," I said and kissed him. "I like you, too."

Monday, June 14, 1976, Locust Hollow—I think I'm falling in love with Jackson. I mean, I really, *really* like him. I think he's adorable; he thinks I'm cute. He likes my ears, which I hate. When I give him head, he grabs hold of my ears to guide my movements. I never thought I'd ever be grateful for my jug-handle ears.

In his quiet unprepossessing way, he notices me. For the first time, I feel seen, even if I can't quite understand what he sees in me. He makes me feel special, though. Our grandfather has drummed into my head that I am not special, not remarkable. And yet Jackson says I am.

Sunday, July 4, 1976, Locust Hollow—I saw Jackson's orange truck, like a rising sun, crest the hill leading to the farm road. Jackson and his family live better than most of the town. I suppose that's possible when you get a tenth of what your congregation—which amounts to most of the town—earns. I don't resent his father, the shepherd, for fleecing his flock, though. This is what you do when you are a shepherd—whether for a wealthy rancher or the Lord. And for the most part, Reverend Jack's congregants seem proud of his higher standard of living and continue to tithe so that it might continue and be sustained.

Anyway, that means Jackson can afford his own vehicle, and battered though it is, it gives us a bit of freedom we wouldn't enjoy otherwise.

As I stood in the yard, waiting for him, I watched my brothers and my grandfather tossing around a football. I had no desire to join them. None. But I did watch with wonder at their easy camaraderie, at their *commonality*. My brothers look like our grandfather. I've noticed their resemblance before, but today, it really struck me how much my brothers look like him. With their short, wide faces and prominent chins, they look like Cro-Magnons. Like him, they are short but powerfully built. Also like him, their skin is ashy from farm work and neglect, and their perpetually unbrushed hair resembles peas scattered across a kitchen floor. How, I wondered again, are we related?

Watching them, though, I couldn't help but marvel at their sheer physicality, brutish as it is, and at their easy machismo that seems enough to make my grandfather favor them over me.

Today, Jackson and I were going to the Fourth of July parade in the next county over. It is America's 200ᵗʰ birthday, and the entire country has contracted bicentennial fever. Never before have the stars and stripes been so widely used and abused. There is fevered talk seeing tall masted celebratory ships. Even Reverend Jack has succumbed, wearing a red, white, and blue stole this morning as he prayed for "God's great country," then dismissed us early so we could enjoy the nation's great birthday celebration.

So, I suppose I shouldn't have been surprised when Jackson drove up wearing a stars-and-stripes neckerchief. But I was flummoxed when he reached into the glovebox and pulled out a matching neckerchief for me.

Wednesday, July 14, 1976, Locust Hollow—Today being Wednesday, Jackson's mother and Reverend Jack had Bible Study, so we had his house to ourselves. We had intercourse for the first time tonight. For months we've been afraid, convincing ourselves we were satisfied with just kissing and being able to sit shoulder to shoulder or touch each other's arm or leg without risking being called a faggot or accused of unauthorized invasion of personal space. There have been, of course, hand jobs, and we've given each other head, but we felt there was more, that we were ready for more. We just weren't sure what that more was.

I thought back over the confusing irrelevance that passed for sex education in the hinterlands, for a moment passing back into that overheated darkened classroom, the students a mix of perplexed—I was one of them—and embarrassed; the teacher red-faced at the front of the room, Reverend Jack pacing and scowling at the back. I tried to remember what I'd learned, while Jackson peered anxiously at me. Then I remembered. There seemed to be two inescapable consequences of sex: pregnancy and syphilis.

As I knew I couldn't get pregnant—I'd gleaned that much from sex ed—I'd believed I had syphilis for a whole year after Juan. I am sure of Jackson, sure that I love him. Everything else, though, is unknown, a crapshoot.

I was thinking about all this when Jackson suddenly said, "I think I want to fuck you."

"OK," I said, relieved we'd at least figured out what to do.

When spit and persuasion proved itself an unsuitable means of lubrication, we swiped butter from a churn. When my orgasm shot from my body, Jackson expressed his astonishment that the one "being done" could feel pleasure. He'd assumed we'd need to take turns "doing" each other. Nope, I was good. Feeling him moving inside me felt amazing, and I recognized on some level that is what I'd always wanted, even though I wasn't sure it was possible.

"Why's your navel sunken?" Jackson asked, propping up on his elbows and tracing the edge of my navel with his finger, tickling me. With a tissue, he mopped up the little puddle of come pooled there.

"Most people's are," I said.

He peered closely at my now-clean navel. "It looks like every picture I've ever seen of the man in the moon," he said.

"I know," I responded. "When I was little, I thought it *was* the man in the moon. I'd spend all day puffing out my stomach to return him to the sky before night came and it was discovered he was missing, that I had him."

He laughed. "You're silly."

"I was *four*," I said indignantly.

"You're still silly," he reassured me. He stuck his tongue in my navel.

I pushed his head away. "And you still have an outie!"

Sunday, September 5, 1976, Locust Hollow—I've poured everything that loving Rio—and to an extent, Juan—had roused in me at Jackson's feet. As my love seems to flow over and around him, he seems to float in it as if he is bathing in the Dead Sea. And he is radiant. For his part, he has pulled me into those waters beside him. For the first time, I know joy and carelessness.

So, I suppose it shouldn't have been a surprise when today he said, "I love you, O."

"And I, you," I responded.

Now, lying in bed alone, thinking of him, I can hear our words rushing through the air and across the dark and separating miles between us. *I love you, O. And I, you.* The words echo around the valley's basin and in our hearts like a lullaby, sending us both separately but happily to sleep.

Saturday, September 25, 1976, Locust Hollow—"Where are you going?" my grandfather demanded.

"To meet Jackson."

"You'd better watch yourself!"

"What? What are you talking about?"

"You think I don't know? You think I'm a fool?"

When I said nothing, my grandfather continued, "First it was that wetback up at the orchard. You following him around all picking season like a lost puppy. And now you're trying to poison Reverend Jack's son with your filth. Don't think you're fooling anybody. Your schoolmates all know and are telling everyone you're freaks."

I remained silent, though I was trembling. I thought it was ironic that our classmates had insisted Jackson, the preacher's kid, was a spy for Jesus when, as it turned out, he was the one being spied on and reported. God, the great jokester in the sky!

"You need to stay away from that boy, or you're going straight to hell."

"I'm already there. If this town isn't hell, I don't know—"

His slap was swift and hard; I swear I felt my teeth rattle in my head. I quickly ran my tongue around the inside of my mouth. No loose teeth.

"I will not have an invert under my roof. I will not have everyone laughing behind my back. I raised you—"

"Reared. You raise chickens. You rear children."

"You think you're so damned smart. That's why no one likes you. That's why everyone thinks you're an invert," he snapped astonishingly, as if speaking proper English was suspect, proof of sin.

"That's fine," I said mildly, with a learned casualness that I knew he found maddening. "I don't like any of you either." And I didn't. How had I ended up in this tribe of savages, ignorant and rude, complacent in their ignorance, in the smallness of their dreams—a good crop, more female chicks than male, a new transistor radio for the kitchen?

That's when he punched me in my face. I lost vision in one eye for some minutes as the capillaries beneath my skin burst; blood poured from my split lip. I could hear my brothers' laughter somewhere behind me.

Invert. So, there's another word for me, for what I am. I pulled a bag of frozen peas from the refrigerator to place over my eye. I caught a glimpse of my face in the mirror over the kitchen sink. A black eye like a scarlet letter tattooed my face. The skin around my eye was a reddish-purple in the corner, darkened to black below my eye, and lightened into a yellowish green at the outside edge. For a moment, my grandfather looked shocked, almost on the verge of apologizing. I noticed he too was trembling. He looked at me hard then walked away.

Invert. The word rang in my ears. Refraining from touching my aching face—I refused to give him the satisfaction of knowing just how much he had hurt me—I moved towards the kitchen door, my vision blurring.

Leaving the violence behind, letting it *go*, I got on my bike and concentrated on pedaling as fast as I could downtown where I was meeting Jackson.

The Hollow's town center is presided over by great husks of empty buildings, in front of which gutters choked with leaves and trash overflow, damming rainwater so the streets are smooth lakes of muddy water moving pointlessly to-and-fro, wherever the aimless wind pushes them. I love its ghostliness, its feeling of abandonment. Most afternoons we meet there, arriving separately so as not to be seen together too often. We run gloriously through those restless muddy waters, spraying ourselves and each other with the water's bitter bounty, and feel free. We often come to have sex, privacy and Vaseline being abundant.

When I arrived, Jackson was already there. He touched my face, already swelling, gently. "What happened?" he asked.

"I had a fight with my grandfather."

"He doesn't seem very nice."

"He isn't. In fact, he's awful. I hate him." I'd never allowed myself to think these thoughts, let alone express them to someone else. But I feel safe with Jackson.

"Don't you have any other relatives you could live with—who would be kinder to you?"

"No. My parents were both only children, and my dad's mom died when he was little. And Grampy Eddie died—he was murdered, actually—a few months before my mom's mother died."

"That's when you moved here, right?"

"Yeah, but really, we left Springfield because of Grampy Eddie. I'm not sure what happened, but after he got killed, my dad said there were mean people who might try to hurt us now that Grampy Eddie wasn't around to protect us, so we should make ourselves scarce for a while. They woke me up early one morning and put me in the back of the Buick Electra Dad inherited from Grampy Eddie and drove us here.

"My parents grew up here. And they went to high school together, which is how they met. My mother was born on the farm. After my dad's mom died, his father put him in the children's home while he went off to Springfield to build a better life for the two of them. My father never said much about the orphanage except that he had been taught how to clean and cook and sew—all things he taught me—so he could help take care of the younger children.

"A month after he graduated high school, Grampy Eddie sent for him to come live in Springfield. By then, Grampy Eddie was a successful numbers man, buying a new Buick every two years and never being seen outside without a fedora and one of his custom-made suits. My mother was devastated my father left but promised she would wait for him. Telling me the story, she said, 'What else could I do? Your dad was the finest boy in Locust Hollow. All the rest were riffraff with no ambition, dirt under their nails, and bad teeth, destined to become potbellied ne'er-do-wells drinking away their Friday and Saturday nights and gambling away their earnings every other night of the week.'

"My father got drafted shortly after he moved to Springfield. By the time he returned from the army, Grampy Eddie had moved to a swanky building with a doorman on the Grand Concourse, where he rented an apartment big enough for three. My father sent for my mother, and they were married a few months later. They lived in the apartment with Grampy Eddie until a few months after I was born, when he moved into a separate suite of rooms off the kitchen that had been, during the building's heyday, the servants' quarters."

"What was your fight with your grandfather about?" Jackson asked, suddenly switching topics.

I shrugged.

"Was it about me?"

I nodded.

"Want to talk about it?"

"No," I said. "But I learned there's a word for what we are. Invert." I could hear the bitterness in my own voice.

Jackson winced. "That's an ugly word. The correct word for us is homosexual. Though a lot of us prefer the term gay."

I was surprised Jackson seemed to know so much. It turns out having his truck gives him the freedom to go to other nearby towns with bigger libraries and a more open-minded populace. He's read about gays in *Time* and *Newsweek* and has even read James Baldwin's *Giovanni's Room*.

Jackson handed me a towel from the back of his truck so we could towel off the water we splashed on ourselves riding my bike through the town center's perpetual puddles.

"Shit! I forgot my lotion," I said, knowing my dry skin would irritate me all the way home. Jackson reached into his glovebox and pulled out a small jar of Lubriderm lotion. When he handed it to me, I looked at him in surprise.

"What? I know you lotion a lot, so I thought having a jar on hand couldn't hurt."

I nearly cried.

"C'mon," he said. "We'll put your bike in back and I'll drive you to the farm road, then you can ride home from there."

Jackson parked at the end of the road leading to the farm. "I wish we could just keep driving and find someplace quiet and live together," he said. Before I could say anything, he kissed me goodbye, then he lifted my bike out of the back of his truck. I waved at his taillights and hopped on my bike, and we each headed home. My face didn't burn as much.

When I got to the farmhouse, it was dark. Soon enough, it would be morning, and dust would fall from the hills above and rise from the valley below, faithful as the sunrise.

YELLOW (1977)

Sunday, January 2, 1977, Locust Hollow—Like Carole King, I feel the earth move under my feet whenever Jackson looks my way—in the hall as we rush to our different classes, at church from across the aisle when he raises a wicked eyebrow at his father's sermon. The sky doesn't come tumbling down, though; instead, it seems to go brighter whenever he is around. Jackson and I have grown closer. And it's becoming obvious to folks how close we've become. We are inseparable. Though we were mostly ignored by our classmates before, now they seem keenly interested in us. They whisper about us, as if we cannot hear them: *they go with boys.* "What *boys*?" Jackson and I wonder. There are only the two of us. We are all we have.

We haven't been too concerned about the whispers and speculation. That is until this morning in church. When Reverend Jack called sinners to the front to confess their sins and repent, my grandfather rose and pulled me to my feet. I stood bewildered as he pushed me into the aisle and toward the front of the church, where Reverend Jack stood like a storm cloud about to release a bolt of lightning. On the other side of the church, Jackson's mother pushed him to his feet and into the aisle. With their hands on our shoulders, my grandfather and Jackson's mother pushed us to our knees.

Reverend Jack called out the demon possessing us, urged us to repent our sin and pledge to return to the path of righteousness. He named neither the demon nor the sin; neither did he assign a name to the path we'd strayed onto.

Two weeks ago, Reverend Jack, from the pulpit, had thundered about the sin and scourge of homosexuality.

"That *word* is the sin," Jackson had whispered to me.

"I hate it, too," I'd whispered back.

Now, I wondered why Reverend Jack was holding back, why he was refusing to name the obvious thing. I glanced over at Jackson, who looked terrified. Praying no one would notice, I reached over and squeezed his hand before quickly drawing it back to my side. My prayer was in vain. The organist's tempo increased; the drums grew louder; the prayers grew more fevered; one of the deaconesses swaying in the aisles fainted.

The praying over us wasn't the worst part, though. The worst part was the "laying on of hands." Hands from every direction, so many hands. Touching us, clutching, grabbing, as if they would tear us to pieces.

Finally, we were allowed to return to our respective pews, while other, lesser sinners replaced us in front of Reverend Jack.

After service, we met, out of sight, in the field behind the church, shaken if not chastened. Jackson stumbled into my arms. We held on tight to each other until our heartbeats slowed, until we were able to speak again.

Thursday, January 20, 1977, Locust Hollow—His truck wheezed, shuddered, and came to a halt as Jackson guided it to the curb; steam rose from under the hood.

"Overheated," he sighed. "Again."

The old truck was leaking coolant. Jackson was waiting till he had enough money saved to fix it. He refused my offer to pay for it, knowing I was saving for college in the fall.

"We just have to wait for it to cool, so I can add more coolant," he explained.

I nodded, looking past him at the row of attached houses in front of which we'd halted. The houses, brick-fronted, were wood-framed, stacked tinder boxes waiting for a lit match or a carelessly discarded cigarette. When one went up in flames, the others fell as well. It had happened periodically throughout the years. The houses frightened me.

We leaned our heads back against the bench seat and leaned towards each other. I was just starting to drift into sleep when I heard what would turn out to be a broom being beaten against the side of the truck. Jackson leapt from the cab, grabbed the broom.

"Miss Lurene, what are you doing?" he demanded.

Lurene paused in her efforts, apparently recognizing him. "I'm sweeping away sin," she shouted, her chin jutting forward.

"What are you talking about?"

"I—I saw you," she spluttered, then lowering her voice, "doing unnatural things with he—" and now she pointed her broom at me. "That spawn of the devil hisself!"

"What are you talking about? My truck overheated. We're just waiting for it to cool down so we can keep driving."

"Why are you—*a preacher's son*—running around with that filthy boy? It ain't right."

"Now Miss Lurene, you know the Lord doesn't think any of us is filthy—not if we have love in our hearts. And Oren here has more love in his heart than just about anybody in this town."

She looked less sure of herself. "Get moving," she spat, "before I have to get Lidell to come out here."

"Now Miss Lurene, wasn't it just last Sunday Reverend Jack talked about being hospitable to folks in need? I know you heard him. I saw you nodding your head and shaking your tambourine. How ashamed of you do you think he'd be right now?"

Lurene looked absolutely cowed. She lowered the broom and, muttering, walked back to her tinderbox house but not before giving me the stink eye.

Climbing back into the cab and slamming the door, Jackson said, "I see why you hate this town. And everyone in it."

"Not everyone. I don't hate you," I said.

"Or Rio," he said wryly.

I looked at him. I wondered if he was jealous. He had no reason to be. Rio was a dream; Jackson was the dream made flesh.

"Why not?" Jackson asked.

"Why not what?"

"Why don't you hate me like you hate everyone else?"

"Do you really not know how special you are?" I asked. "Everyone in this town is the same, believes the same things. It's like they're all cut from the same dull pattern and living according to some sort of mass-produced template. But you—you're different, rare. I was waiting for you to show up, without even knowing it. Someone like you only shows up once in a great while." I fell silent then. "Blue Moon," I whispered, speaking again. "You're my Blue Moon."

"What's a Blue Moon?"

I sat up and wiggled my fingers against his. "The moon cycles through phases that last about a month, so there are typically twelve moons in a year. But the moon's phases actually take twenty-nine and a half days to complete. If you do the math, you'll see it takes just three hundred and fifty-four days to complete twelve lunar cycles. So, every two and a half years or so, there's a thirteenth moon within a calendar year. That moon is called a Blue Moon. You are my Blue Moon."

"Are you making that up?"

"No. Don't you believe me?"

"'Course I do. "Now I believe in something new, in something I didn't know existed. I believe in you, Oren."

Monday, February 14, 1977, Locust Hollow—Today is Valentine's Day—our first together. Jackson makes me happy. It doesn't matter what we're doing; as long as we're together, I'm happy. This is quite a different feeling from the hot passion I feel when I look at him, when we touch.

Somehow, he has opened up long-forgotten memories. Even though I try not to dwell on the past—for I find that memory can become like Prometheus's eagle—I can't help remembering.

Early on, before the arrival of my brothers, before the drinking and shouting began, my mother had been my favorite person. As long as I was with her, I was happy. Closing my eyes now, I can catch glimpses of us back then—making peanut brittle together

LARRY BENJAMIN

in our sun-splashed kitchen that was painted bright yellow; her chasing me along the bank of a river, playing hide-and-seek in the trees.

I remember my parents' anniversary party, the last party they had before we left Springfield. I can still see Dad standing, a whiskey sour in one hand, a cigarette in the other, wearing a sportscoat with suede elbow patches, watching my mother floating through the crowd in a navy-blue-and-orange chevron-patterned sheath dress, offering hors d'oeuvres and wine and gracious thank-you-for-comings. The adults in the living room held drinks while dancing to the stacked 45s, which dropped to the turntable in turn: Miriam Makeba's "Pata Pata," Hugh Masekela's "Grazing in the Grass," and my favorite "Wack Wack" by the Young Holt Trio, which all the kids present danced to.

That I was happy before, that Jackson and I have found each other, makes me believe, for the first time, I can be happy again.

Saturday, May 7, 1977, Locust Hollow—Our picnic today was rained out. Rain here tends to be like a toddler's tantrums. It erupts suddenly out of silence and clear skies with a sound like a clapper bell from hell, then a torrent of unstoppable water pours down, eventually stopping as suddenly as it started. Then, as soon as you've gotten used to the silence ringing in your ears, the clapper bell rings, and the storm rages again. Like a toddler's incoherent fury, you are left wondering what in hell has caused it.

Undaunted, we unpacked our picnic in the cab of his truck and holding hands, we ate, talking about everything and nothing, sometimes singing along with our favorite songs on the truck's scratchy AM radio as the storm raged around us.

Sunday, March 20, 1977, Locust Hollow—Each Sunday since January when Reverend Jack prayed over us, someone in church has conspired to separate Jackson and me after service. The conspirators seem legion—the elders, the deaconesses, sometimes a particularly righteous parishioner. So today, we decided to meet up *before* Sunday service—in the orchards behind the church. When I arrived, Jackson was there with Reuben, the choir director. It was impossible to tell what his body looked like under his voluminous choir robe, but his rounded face with its soft features is actually quite attractive. He speaks quietly but plays the piano like a demon.

"I'm glad I caught you boys," he said, pulling a cigarette from a new pack and lighting it. Jackson and I looked at him in astonishment; Father Jack forbids the smoking of cigarettes.

"Why?" Jackson asked.

"I—I wanted to tell you boys—I envy your courage," he said quietly.

"Courage?" Jackson repeated, sounding confused.

"Yeah. Courage—the courage not to let them," he jerked his thumb towards the church, "weaken your devotion to each other. Each Sunday, you stand tall and defiant as they lay their hands on and pray over you. I can see in your faces that your faith in the rightness of your relationship is stronger than their prayers."

"That's not courage," I said.

"You're too young to know what courage is," Reuben said, smiling.

"Oren doesn't care what anyone thinks of him," Jackson said.

"It's not that. It's just that I can only be myself. I don't see the point of pretending to be someone else. I don't understand actors—that

43

seems like the worst job in the world—day after day pretending to be someone else. Always having to speak someone else's words, express someone else's thoughts." I shuddered.

Reuben nodded. "I've noticed you boys trying to slip away after church…"

"It seems like Reverend Jack has summoned a legion to keep us from going off together."

"That's what I really wanted to talk to you about. Starting next Sunday, I'll create a distraction with the recessional hymn so you can slip out unmolested."

Sunday, March 27, 1977, Locust Hollow—Reuben kept his promise. Today, the recessional hymn was so unexpected, powerful, and perfect, the congregation paused their hurried departure to stop and listen as if caught in an enchantment, while Jackson and I slipped away unmolested. The weather was surprisingly mild for March, so we went swimming up at the quarry.

Thursday, April 14, 1977, Locust Hollow—Today, my college acceptance letter arrived. I felt like the long-closed door to my prison cell was finally creaking open. My grandfather came upon me like a shadow. Spying the letter in my hand, knowing I had been waiting for it, seeing the smile on my face, he taunted me.

Pointing at the letter in my hand, he said dismissively, "That makes no never mind. You can't go."

"You can't stop me," I said.

"How you gonna pay for college, boy?"

I could hear Mr. Fabricant's words when I'd asked the same question: *"If you have the will, we will find a way."* I'd had the will, and he'd kept his word. Mr. Fabricant is our French teacher, an unkempt, short man who teaches us French while wearing a tattered putty-colored London Fog trench coat. Most days, he listlessly leads us through declining French verbs and the singing of the French National anthem and "Frere Jacques" all while drunk.

He is a terrible French teacher but proved to be an excellent guide through the thicket of applications, essays, and scholarship requests that lead to college admission.

"I got a scholarship," I said, "and I can work part-time for walking-around money."

I walked away before my grandfather could close his mouth.

Friday, May 13, 1977, Locust Hollow—Tonight was prom. Prom always has a black-and-white color scheme; black-and-white posters and stills from old movies lend a bit of credibility to the scheme, as if it were a deliberate lark rather than a grim necessity. You see, ours is a town where no one has money for prom dresses and rented tuxedos, so prom has always used this color scheme so the girls can wear hand-me-down wedding dresses and the boys' their fathers' old funeral suits. From late winter until early spring, every seamstress and anyone who can thread a needle is pressed into service to transform the wedding dresses of mothers, aunts, and even grandmothers into prom dresses.

Tonight, Jackson and I sat together in a tree and watched our classmates arrive in their recycled finery. Just before the dance started, Reverend Jack—who strongly objects to it each year, dancing being "a vertical expression of a horizontal proposition"— arrived with a contingent of deaconesses in tow; each carried a wooden ruler as if it were a crucifix in the presence of evil.

"What are the rulers for?" I asked Jackson.

"It's to make sure the dancers are at least six inches apart at all times."

I stared at him; he fell onto his back and crossed his arms under his head. I worried he'd fall out of our tree and, curling around him with my head on his chest, wrapped my arms around him.

Of course, Jackson and I didn't go. Going with anyone besides each other was impossible; going together was a bridge too far even for us.

We watched our classmates, paired up boy-girl, boy-girl, marching solemnly with subdued excitement up to the gymnasium. The last to arrive were Rio and his girlfriend, Victoria. She was wrapped in yards of ruffles and tulle—her aunt was a set designer at the community theatre two towns over. Rio, boldly, was wearing his grandfather's zoot suit from the 1940s. Shockingly yellow, it featured high-waisted, wide-legged, tight-cuffed, pegged trousers and a long coat with wide padded shoulders and still wider lapels. On his head, crowning his now-slicked-down hair, was a broad-brimmed yellow hat.

Once everyone was inside, we retreated to the fields that ringed the high school and watched the lights, listened to laughter and music: Andy Gibb's "I Just Want to Be Your Everything," K.C. and The Sunshine Band's "I'm Your Boogie Man," and Natalie Cole's "I've Got Love on My Mind," which really drew the rulers into action, we imagined.

Saturday, June 25, 1977, Locust Hollow—Graduation was yesterday. My grandfather didn't attend. Neither did my brothers. Today, Mr. Fabricant, as is his tradition, had the senior class at his house—an immaculate two-story cottage placed in the middle of an acre of pristine green lawn and bordered in the back by a neat row of apple trees—for a picnic to celebrate our graduation. Mr. Fabricant asked me to help him bring out the homemade sausage and hamburgers for the grill. On the way to the kitchen, I spied his living room, full of plump, white velvet sofas like clouds sealed in clear plastic with gold-colored plastic trim. The tall, iridescent white lamps dripping crystals were capped with tall, white shades wrapped in cellophane. Plastic runners crisscrossed the white shag carpeting like highways through fields of white corn. The wall behind the sofa was mirrored; the other three walls were upholstered in crushed red velvet. It was the most beautiful and pristine room I'd ever seen. I vowed one day I would live in a house like it while I avoided my classmates' curious stares and waited anxiously for Jackson to arrive.

Unable to stop him from attending altogether, Reverend Jack had settled for delaying Jackson's arrival as long as possible to decrease his exposure to Mr. Fabricant's radical ideas and encouragement of free thinking. Reverend Jack didn't approve of Mr. Fabricant encouraging his students to leave Locust Hollow and find their places in the larger world any more than he appreciated Mr. Fabricant's exhortation to examine the beliefs they'd been taught and to discard those beliefs as necessary.

Thursday, August 18, 1977, Locust Hollow—The hallway outside our only bathroom stank of Hai Karate cologne, my clue that my grandfather was going out with one of the several church widows he was making time with. Usually, these dates occurred on Friday and Saturday evening, but the stench was unmistakable and positive proof he had a date.

My grandfather is neither good-looking nor particularly clean and certainly without any discernable charm; still, he's made his way through the widows in the church choir and is now at work on the deaconesses. I guess a man shared is better than no man at all.

Anyway, I knew he was going out and my brothers were already in bed, so it was an opportunity to spend time with Jackson. I called him. We had a signal system set up: when one of us wanted to talk or see the other, one of us would call the other and let the phone ring once then hang up. The other would then call back if it was safe.

We were forced to make love in the dark; we felt like we were dancing in the moonlight. *He goes with boys*, they whispered about each of us, and we hadn't cared. My brothers—that pigeon-shooting, puppy-drowning, football-throwing legion of assholes—discovered Jackson and me in the barn, *in medias res*, at our most vulnerable and defenseless.

My brothers stared at us agog, twittering and giggling, the looks on their faces as difficult to decipher as the sounds they made. My brothers don't speak; instead, they utter a series of shrieks and squawks that vary in pitch and volume, but which are uniformly rhythmic and repetitive, from morning to night. At times, their emissions are quite prolonged and dramatic, making me think they are singing an opera, but instead of French or German, they are singing in a language of their own making.

As Jackson struggled to get dressed under their wide-eyed stares like spotlights, he shouted, "I thought you said they were in bed."

"They *were*," I said, struggling to dress myself. "Get out of here," I shouted at my brothers. "Go back to bed." When they stood still staring, I chased them away with a certain violent gesture and a shout as guttural as the sounds they make.

By the time my grandfather returned, Jackson was safely away, and my brothers and I were in bed. I hoped for sleep, which eluded me until the early hours.

Friday, August 19, 1977, Locust Hollow—Jackson and I hadn't spoken since he rushed away yesterday, after my brothers caught us in the barn, so I was anxious to see him at work today.

Jackson works at Lewisohn's like I do, but while I work the sales floor and the registers, he works as the "receiver"—unloading deliveries and sweeping and mopping and cleaning the bathrooms. So, we don't work together, but Mr. Lewisohn lets us take our breaks together. We don't know if he's oblivious to the rumors about us or if, as the lone Jews in Locust Hollow, he and his bookkeeper wife are inclined to cut us some slack since we share the same pain of exclusion.

Jackson was pacing in the breakroom when I arrived. "Sunday is gonna be a shitshow," he said.

I shrugged. "It always is. They'll pray over us, put their hands on us. They've done it before."

"They're gonna send us to camp," he blurted, pausing in his perambulations.

"Camp?"

"In the mountains! They'll make us sleep outside and pump our own water."

"Huh?"

"They're going to send us to a camp to make us straight." He began pacing again.

"What? That's just stupid," I said.

"They're gonna do it!"

"How do you know this?" I asked. He stopped in front of me.

"My mother told me. I don't think she meant to. It just sort of slipped out."

His mother, Esther, is a thin wan woman who always walks behind her husband; she is little more than his wife, an obligation or maybe an expectation. She follows behind Reverend Jack like an early morning shadow and is as insubstantial; she offers little comfort to Jackson and none to anyone else.

"Your brothers ratted us out."

"How? They don't speak."

"Apparently, they do. Maybe that gibberish they speak is some sort of secret language only they and your grandfather understand— I don't know—but they told your grandfather, and he went to my father, who now wants to send us both to that camp."

I saw an immediate future of electroshock treatments, perhaps a lobotomy, beatings with a specially consecrated Bible while we were naked and wet. I would survive; Jackson, for all his defiance and masculine vigor, would not. He was like a dancing, celebratory flame on a candle wick—all it would take was a pair of spit-damped fingers to snuff him out.

When I remained quiet, Jackson resumed his aimless, troubled walking.

"Will you stop pacing?" I snapped. "I'm trying to think."

Jackson paused his movements and looked at me hopefully. He hadn't looked this hopeful since the day he'd told me he liked me and asked me out on a date. "Look," I said, "we've graduated. I start college in a few weeks. You can come with me."

"What?"

We hadn't talked about it. I think we'd both assumed this—*we*— would end once I left for college. Jackson had made no plans for after graduation; it was almost as if he hadn't expected to graduate after twelve years. He insists he isn't college material. "And I don't want to go to Bible college for sure—"

"Bible college?" I asked.

"Reverend Jack wants me to go. He wants me to take over his ministry."

"I can't see you in Bible college," I said.

"Me either. You want me to go to college, though, don't you?"

"I don't want you to do anything but be you—and love me. I don't agree that you're not 'college material.' It's more that you don't *want* to go to college, which is fine, by the way. You just need to figure out what *you* want to do and do that."

He said he'd thought about joining the army to escape what he calls the town's "Jesus Fever," and the claustrophobia of being a preacher's kid. He'd miss me, he said, and the army might give him some perspective, some other things to think about while letting him see the world, experience life in other places free of the pall of fire and brimstone and the false promise of salvation as he learned to live without me.

I know ours will never be considered a legendary romance. No one will write a song or even a poem about us; we are too ordinary, too prosaic, but we have loved each other, lifted each other up, fought and struggled to stay together. We have each, separately, dreamed the impossible dream of loving and being loved in return, and we are. I suddenly realized I couldn't— *wouldn't*—leave Jackson behind.

"Look, I have a work-study job and a housing allowance. You probably can't live with me on campus, but we could get an off-campus apartment. You could get a job."

"You want me to go with you?"

"Yeah," I said, "but only if you want to—"

He hugged me then, lifting me off my feet. Just as Mrs. Lewisohn pushed open the door to the breakroom.

Saturday, August 20, 1977, Locust Hollow—Jackson and I plan to leave tomorrow right before church, so this morning, I went to the bank to close my accounts. I got up early because technically, the bank is open until noon on Saturdays, but sometimes Fontella Bass, the lone teller, closes early to get her hair done or because she's bored. It's usually not a problem, though, because folks just call up the bank manager and he goes down and reopens the bank.

I handed Fontella my bank slip; I was withdrawing two hundred and fifty dollars in cash and taking the rest as a money order and closing my account.

"I hear that Mr. Fabricant down at the high school has been encouraging kids to apply to college. Sounds kinda uppity to me—and he should know better. Kids from these here parts,

people like us aren't meant to be 'sociating with college folk—
even Reverend Jack says so—never mind attending college
alongside them."

Fontella ran out of steam as I ran out of patience with her stream-
of-consciousness rambling. She looked at my withdrawal slips.
"Oh! These withdrawals will close your account. You don't want
to do that," she said, pushing a fresh withdrawal slip towards me.

"Why wouldn't I want to do that?"

"You listen to me. That Mr. Fabricant has filled your head with
nonsense dreams of glory. Dreams and glory are for other people.
Once you're in the city, you'll miss us and our quiet ways."

I'd miss no one, I knew, except Rio maybe. Rio. Handsome,
popular, distant Rio. My singular obsession until Jackson came
along. Though our interactions had been few and far between,
he'd always been kind to me. Once, he'd draped an arm across
my shoulders, until a group of equally popular boys called him
away. My shoulder had burned where his arm had lain; a week
later, the sensation, like a sunburn, peeled away leaving just
a depth of feeling and the shadow of a smile.

Fontella was still talking, advising, when I tuned back in. "You
listen to me. Leave some money in this account so when you
come back with your tail between your legs—"

"I'm not coming back," I said. "So, either give me my money or
I'm going to call the bank manager, who will."

I'd grown up around these people, and I tried to be respectful,
but I was at my wits' end. Just the *idea* of being forced to stay
in Locust Hollow at this point would destroy me and Jackson.
To my relief, she handed me my cash and money order without
another word. I stuffed everything into the front pocket of my

dungarees and headed out to my bike, which I'd left lying on the sidewalk outside. I pedaled around the block to calm down, and as I passed the bank, I saw Fontella turn over the "closed" sign and lock the doors. It was 10:15.

When I got back to the farm, I called Jackson. We agreed not to see or talk to each other until we meet up to leave tomorrow so, as we'd planned, I called his house, let the phone ring once, then hung up and called back, letting the phone ring once more before hanging up so he'd know my trip to the bank had been successful.

Sunday, August 21, 1977, Locust Hollow—"Why aren't you dressed for church?" my grandfather demanded, coming upon me as I stood, my back to the sink, eating a bowl of cereal.

"I'm not going," I said.

He lunged at me, grabbed, and twisted my ear savagely. "Yes, you are."

"Why?" I asked, struggling against the pain. "Going to church isn't going to make me what you think a man is, any more than going makes you a Christian."

His slap was swift and stinging. I could feel a bruise rising. My skin was as sensitive as I was; another of my failings as a man. The cereal bowl fell from my hands and smashed on the stone floor; milk, like blood, flowed around my feet.

"Look what you done!" My grandfather lunged at me again.

I reached behind me and grabbed the Brown's soda bottle that stood on the drain board waiting to be turned in for a penny. I smashed it against the cast iron sink. At that moment, I ceased being a child, anyone's child. Wielding the broken neck of the bottle, I taunted him. "Come on. Hit me again."

My grandfather fell back a step; his mouth hung open a little. "I never thought I'd live to see the day a child of mine would raise his hands against me."

I laughed a little. "I am no one's child and certainly not yours. You have always beaten me as if I was a man. Today, if you raise a hand against me, I will kill you like a man."

I could see my brothers gathered in the doorway to the kitchen looking confused and a little frightened. Still holding the bottle like a torch lighting a dark path, I slipped my backpack awkwardly over my left shoulder and picked up my suitcase. He seemed to notice my luggage for the first time.

"What?" he asked, confused, but he stepped to the side and my brothers parted, allowing me to pass between them. Outside, I threw the bottle to the ground and spit in the dust. I could see Jackson in his battered pickup truck waiting for me on the road at the edge of my grandfather's property.

I retrieved the box I'd placed in the crush of corn plants clustered beside the driveway. In the box was all I had left of my parents: their wedding album, my father's Henry Mancini albums and a half-empty bottle of my mother's favorite perfume, Wind Song by Prince Matchabelli. I'd once had a Laguiole penknife with a rosewood handle that my father had given me the summer we moved to the farm when I was seven. His father had given it to him when he himself was seven. It was my most treasured possession. I'd kept it hidden with all my childhood treasures in a shoebox secreted under a loose floorboard beneath my bed; only my dad had known where I kept it. The morning after my parents died, I went to look for it, hoping it would bring me comfort, but it wasn't in its hiding place.

I hoisted the box into the bed of Jackson's truck, which already held his backpack, an old suitcase and two orange milk crates containing his collection of clocks. Friday night, after we'd gotten off work at Lewisohn's, Jackson had parked at the edge of the woods so we could finalize our escape plan. After our plan was firm, he'd given me the moon and the stars in that truck bed. I threw my suitcase and knapsack next to his and walked around to the passenger door. When I got in, he reached out and rubbed my knee. I smiled at him, but neither of us spoke.

When we reached the outskirts of town, Jackson pulled onto the shoulder of the road. He threw the stick shift with its bulbous wooden head into neutral. He stared straight ahead. The sky was gray; the sun, visible along the rims of the slow-moving clouds, burned bright, making the very air glitter like metal; the road that stretched before us seemed less dusty than the one beneath us. His hands gripped the steering wheel so tightly the veins rose angry and green from his thin skin.

"Are you sure," Jackson asked, "that we can do this?"

Through the side mirror, I could see the soot-blackened houses we were about to leave behind, the result of a populace who had, all at once, abandoned as futile the practice of whitewashing their fences and cottages and farmhouses under the constant assault of the factories two towns over, a veritable Mt Vesuvius that breathed soot into the air six-to-six, six days a week. Today, as every Sunday I could remember, a phalanx of grimy workers with their slowly blackening lungs moved in twos and threes and families to the graying steepled church to give thanks. *For what?*

For years, I'd seen them on Sundays when they filed into Reverend Jack's church in their fraying Sunday best with their gray faces and black lungs; they brought with them the stink of the factory, reminding us, and themselves, that Monday was just around the corner. I wouldn't, I knew, see them again for a long time, if ever.

"I'm sure, "I said. "We *can* do this.

Jackson nodded without looking at me and moved the truck into gear.

One of my most enduring memories is of a dog who lived on the farm. I suppose she was my grandfather's dog, though he didn't seem particularly fond of her. She was a nondescript black mutt, sweet as the day was long. She didn't even have a name. She disappeared once for a week. One of my brothers found her after a neighbor complained of a stray black dog that had given birth in his barn. My brother led my grandfather and my other brothers and me to the neighbor's barn. My grandfather gathered the puppies in a burlap flour sack to carry them back to the farm. Once back at the farm, he filled a large tin basin with water and pulling one black-and-pink pup from the pile of squirming newborns held it under water until the air bubbles stopped. He then invited each of my brothers to do the same. I hid in the hayloft stifling my screams in a bale of hay. When the last puppy had stopped squirming and been tossed into a pile with the other still puppies, our dog walked slowly over and nudged the pile of still-warm flesh that had seemingly been her life's work, her pride and joy in a mostly joyless life. She turned and regarded my grandfather and my brothers, who stood still, pinned, and mildly alarmed by her baleful glare and guttural growl. Suddenly she turned away and walked out of that barn. She didn't once look back. We never saw her again.

As Jackson pulled away, I looked at the receding farm in the rearview mirror. I realized that if the farm burned to the ground tomorrow, it wouldn't matter to me because everything

I cherished—everything that was important to me—was in Jackson's truck with me.

Monday, August 22, 1977, University City—As the road we were on became paved, and widened into two, then three lanes, and streetlights appeared along the shoulders, I began to relax. I imagined the camp folks sitting in their white panel van in the empty, dusty, weed-choked lot that passed for the church parking lot—no one drove to services, few having cars and most living within walking distance—beside the church. I began to imagine them falling in on themselves as if by Jackson and I evading their clutches, we'd managed to drop a house on them.

Around midday, we stopped to eat at a McDonald's. We were hesitant, unsure; neither of us had ever eaten "fast food" before, but we were hungry. We stared up at the illuminated menu with its glossy photos of plump juicy hamburgers and something called chicken nuggets that didn't look like any part of a chicken we'd ever seen. We ordered burgers and French fries that looked like long, soft pieces of balsa wood. It was the first time we'd ever eaten a meal that no one we knew prepared; that we didn't know who the meat came from; that we ate a meal without vegetables, without a glass of milk.

We slept in Jackson's truck last night at the edge of campus, which was still and dark by the time we arrived.

"Are you sure this is OK?" I asked Jackson. "Are you sure *you're,* OK? Do you need anything?" The calm I had felt as we left Locust Hollow behind now disappeared in the cramped confines of the cab of Jackson's truck in this dark, unfamiliar city.

"You're here," Jackson said. "You're all I need."

Seconds later, his head resting on my shoulder, he was asleep. My pounding heart felt like it would punch a hole in my chest. His gentle, rhythmic snoring eventually calmed me, and I too fell asleep. I dreamt my heart had beat a hole in my chest and fallen out. Jackson caught the throbbing, bloody muscle in his hand and returned it to its place in my chest, sealing the opening by pressing his chest against mine. I woke to the rhythm of Jackson's chest rising and falling against mine.

Friday, September 30, 1977, University City—We spent three days sleeping in the cab of Jackson's truck. We showered at the university gym—my student ID allowed me and a guest to use the facilities—and we ate at a diner. Neither one of us had ever eaten in a diner before. I was amazed that you could order breakfast at any time and mostly ordered fat sunny yellow omelets stuffed with peppers and sausage like my mother used to make.

The people at student housing didn't seem at all curious about our relationship, only wanting to get us "off the street," going so far as to call the landlord and urging him to make an apartment immediately available to us. Our new home is a small, furnished, one-bedroom apartment on the ground floor of a crumbling Victorian rowhouse, which is missing a great deal of its gingerbread trim painted in a flaking, faded yellow that had probably once been as bright and promising as a new school bus on the first day of school. To Jackson and me, it was the Taj Mahal and Buckingham Palace rolled into one. Right after we unloaded our possessions, we went to Woolworth's and bought towels and sheets for our full-size bed; everything else came with the apartment.

Jackson got a job in construction and another one delivering the *Wall Street Journal* to office buildings and apartments downtown. My scholarship includes a work-study job that pays slightly more than minimum wage, so I now work at student housing twenty hours a week. If my grades are good at the end of the semester, I'll be eligible to work more hours. I also got a job waiting tables a few evenings a week and Saturdays at a cuchifritos restaurant in the Puerto Rican and Dominican neighborhood that borders campus. I like the job a lot. The restaurant is much grander than the converted bus in Locust Hollow, with colorful lighting and big, flashy signs that are as enticing as the smells wafting into the street. It is always busy. But the smells, the sounds, the people, the menu—bacalaitos, morcilla, papas rellenas, jibaro en canoa—remind me of picking season, of Juan, of Rio.

Thursday, October 27, 1977, University City—This is heaven—though can someone like me who thoroughly rejects religion reliably write of heaven? But how else to describe this…freedom, this absence of judgment? No more hurried caresses or stolen kisses or scrambling out of bed lest we get caught. Affection is no longer forced to be circumspect or hidden altogether; sex, at all hours of the day and night, is as loud as it needs to be.

I realize this is to an extent a false freedom, like living in a zoo preserve that faithfully approximates your natural habitat but is still a confining enclosure. We still get disapproving glances, and it's not like we'll be going to city hall to get a marriage license. Still, it feels good to soar free. Even on clipped wings.

Jackson says that after Locust Hollow, University City feels like Graceland. This crowded city of strangers has granted us grace—grace to be ourselves, grace to love each other how we want, grace that the people we grew up with and around united to deny us.

Grace has changed for us in ways big and small, or maybe they are all small ways that seem big to us: when we're on South Street, we can walk with our arms around each other; people don't fall silent as we approach, then start to whisper once we have passed; we can call each other boyfriend; the threat of fire and brimstone no longer hangs over our embraces; old men ask to buy us drinks when we're out. We always refuse. It seems untoward for men in their thirties to be buying drinks for a pair of eighteen-year-olds.

We went out to dinner to celebrate my birthday; we had a gay waiter. He was gay as a sun-dappled meadow, its wild grasses dancing wantonly, like a heathen naked, in the sunlight. "Y'all are so cute," he cooed before seating us in a corner in the dark in the back—"A booth made for romance," he announced.

Jackson ordered a tonic water and sipped it as if it was a very strong gin, as if the cocktail mixer itself was a first cousin to the devil's brew. And that is I why I love him, my PK, my preacher's kid. Once, lying with my head in his lap, I'd asked him how it was that he, a preacher's kid had managed to love me, overruling his father's will. He'd stroked my hair and said, "Easy. My love for you is stronger than Daddy's hate for what my loving you makes me."

Saturday, November 19, 1977, University City—Our new life is intruded upon weekly when Jackson receives a letter from his parents. These missives are full of prayers and denunciations and entreaties to leave me behind and return home, to return to the path God hacked out of the Garden. Though the *Camp* is never mentioned, it remains an implicit threat, a trap. Jackson has stopped writing back. He now leaves their letters unread in a pile on the kitchen table, and when he can't seem to stand the sight of them anymore, he tosses the pile into the trash.

So yesterday, when a letter from his parents came—this one written in a female hand, I was surprised when he opened it. As often happens when he gets one of their letters, he grew distant. With sleep, he was restless. Eventually, he rolled into my arms and settled, as if he, lost in the desert, stumbling, had located me, his North Star high above his head, and followed me home to safety. By morning, his melancholy dissolved like a ripple on a pond.

I have not heard from my grandfather or my brothers once. But Jackson and I live through and for each other, so I do not feel their absence. I wonder sometimes if he misses his parents.

Saturday, December 24, 1977, University City—Jackson's parents called today. Thinking they were calling to wish us a Merry Christmas, Jackson held the receiver between us. After Reverend Jack stomped and shouted through a "prayer for the season" without wishing Jackson Merry Christmas, he passed the phone to his wife. In her near whisper, her shadow's voice, she asked about our apartment. When she learned there was only one bedroom, she asked if there was really room for two beds. "No," Jackson said. "There's only room for one bed."

"So where does *the other one* sleep? In the living room?"

She always refers to me as "the other one." As if I don't have a name.

"He has a name," Jackson said. "It's Oren. And no, he doesn't sleep in the living room. We have a full-size bed, so—"

She pounced with all the triumph of the holiday season. "See! If you'd come home, you'd have your own bed!"

We looked at each other. Having heard enough, I walked away.

"Merry Christmas, Ma," Jackson said and hung up the phone.

After he had calmed down, I asked, "Why did you just hang up instead of explaining our relationship?"

"She wouldn't understand," Jackson said. "She and my father have always slept in separate beds in separate rooms."

"They do? Why?"

He shrugged. "I don't know. Something to do with Reverend Jack needing nights alone with his thoughts and God."

Reverend Jack treated his wife not as a wife but like a disciple. I wondered for the first time if the bright, burning flame in Jackson and me that Reverend Jack had so determinedly prayed to extinguish also burned within him; I wondered if his outrage and moral condemnation of us was just the smoke from another fire.

I didn't share these thoughts with Jackson because, despite his vigorous masculinity and intractable determination to be himself, he is pretty fragile. I was afraid that learning that someone like us, like him, had worked so hard to destroy us. *That*, I think, would break him.

Sunday, December 25, 1977, University City—Today was officially our first Christmas together. Jackson gave me a twelve-inch black-and-white TV so I can catch *All My Children* between classes. I gave him a circa 1950s Avalon two-register mechanical chronograph watch to replace the Sears and Roebuck LED digital watch he usually wore. I'd seen it in the window of a pawn shop. It was more than I could afford, but the shop's owner was an old gay guy who clearly fancied me. I'd exploited his lust to negotiate the price down. Wrapping the watch, he asked me with feigned casualness who the watch was for.

"My boyfriend," I told him. He seemed crushed. I felt bad. When he handed me the bag and said sadly, but sweetly, "I wish you both a Merry Christmas," I felt worse.

When Jackson unwrapped the watch, he blinked at it rapidly and looked from me to the watch and back again. "This is for me? Really?"

I nodded. "And it even works," I teased.

"This is the best gift I've ever gotten," he said. When he wrapped his arms around me, I leaned against him. My feelings about exploiting the old guy at the pawn shop evaporated. I would, I knew, do anything to secure Jackson's happiness.

GREEN (1978)

Wednesday, January 18, 1978, University City—Mary Jane— henceforth to be known as MJ—is one of the first friends I made here in our new life. A thin athletic girl with short, bobbed hair, her wardrobe seems to consist entirely of worn coveralls, which she wears everywhere, paired with large diamond earrings and a Cartier tank watch. She is a walking contradiction. We're both in the School of Communications so we have a lot of the same classes. The day we met last semester, she ran after me after one of our shared classes. "Hey, wait up," she called. I stopped walking. When she caught up to me, she said, "I've noticed we have a lot of the same classes including the next one so I thought we could walk together."

When I said nothing, she seemed to falter. "You're Oren, right?"

"Yes."

"I'm Mary Jane, but I prefer MJ. Only my parents call me Mary Jane."

I nodded, wondering why this bright pixie of a girl dressed in green denim overalls was talking to me.

She tried again. "Is it OK if we walk to class together?"

I shrugged and she fell into step beside me. I guess she was unnerved by my silence because she suddenly asked, "So, Oren, where did you grow up? I can tell you're not from around here."

"On a farm—my grandfather's farm."

"So, you were raised by your grandfather?"

Reared. I started to correct her, thought better of it. I was unsure how to answer her. I don't feel anyone, least of all my grandfather, reared me. I feel more like I reared myself, pulling myself, like a wounded wolf in a forest, from milestone to milestone.

"Yes," I said.

"Don't you have parents?"

"They died."

"Oh. I'm so sorry—"

"Don't be. It was a long time ago."

My parents had been driving the Buick Electra 225—Grampy Eddie's beloved "deuce and a quarter." They were also drunk. The Electra collided with a tanker truck making a late delivery to Locust Hollow's only gas station and exploded. We'd buried what we could find of them—rags, teeth, bones, a hank of hair— and pretended they'd been whole in their caskets. I can still see Reverend Jack in his sooty cassock standing over my parents' grave and thundering about sin and retribution but uttering nary a word about forgiveness and redemption. Calming down, he'd concluded the graveside service, "We therefore commit these bodies to the ground, earth to earth, ashes to ashes, dust to dust…"

I'd found it deeply unfair that having been raised in ashes and dust, having returned to the ashes and dust of her childhood the summer before, when my grandmother had died, that again and for all eternity my mother would be consigned to ashes and dust. It had especially hurt because I knew how much she hated moving back to the farm. A few years after we moved to the farm, after my brothers were born, I overheard my mother tell my father, "I hate it here. I blame Eddie."

"Eddie?" my father repeated, sounding puzzled.

"Yes. Eddie. If he hadn't gone and gotten his fool head shot off over a woman, we would never have moved back here."

I'd wanted to hear the rest of their conversation—I was then of an age where I was curious about the world of adults—but being a kid, the need for sleep surpassed my curiosity and I fell asleep before I heard any more.

I no longer remember my parents' faces or the sound of their voices. I do remember the smell of corn whiskey on their breath and, in hard times, the sugary smell of MD 20/20.

"So, you've no other family?" MJ asked.

I thought of my stupid, violent brothers. "No," I said.

"I can't imagine not having a family," she said. "My mom is one of three children, and my dad, Octavio, is eight of nine. I have, like, forty-two cousins. I can't imagine not having family."

When I shrugged, she nudged my shoulder with hers. "Don't worry," she said. "I'll be your family."

"I have Jackson," I said.

"So now you have Jackson *and* me." After a moment, she added, "You can count on me. I'm an only child. I always wanted a brother, though, and now I feel like I have one."

She was so kind, I thought. Vivienne Leigh as Blanche DuBois in *A Streetcar Named Desire* might have always depended on the kindness of strangers, but outside of my parents—for a time, before we moved to the farm—and Jackson, there hasn't been anyone I can count on to show me kindness. And certainly, there were no strangers in Locust Hollow.

"So, you and Jackson...?" MJ queried, interrupting my thoughts.

"What about us?"

She drew a breath, seeming to marshal her strength. "So, are you...like...lovers?"

I looked at her. "We are."

"But he doesn't go to school here?"

"No. He's not the college type. That's why we live off campus."

"Are you two runaways?"

I snorted. "Eighteen-year-olds don't run away. They write themselves new stories," I said looking off into the distance.

Unlike back in Locust Hollow—I refuse to call it "home"; it was never my home; home is where Jackson is—MJ is interested in us, in learning about us. Instead of repeating rumors or speculating, she asks us questions. She doesn't treat us like foul curiosities in a shop window.

When we first met, MJ seemed intrigued by the novelty of two guys so openly paired up, by our easy affection, and seemed to hold us in different esteem. But then the novelty wore off and we are just her friends now.

That's another new thing for us here—friends. There's Faiz and Sue P and Pauline. Pauline is a big-boned girl, buxom, with a washtub-sized ass; she looks like every cartoon figure of a sexpot you've ever seen. She's a freshman like us, but she's twenty-one. "I took a gap year that turned into three," she admits, shrugging charmingly; and Diogenes Alejandro Xenos Sanchez, whose mad romantic mother named him after a character in Harold Robbins' *The Adventurers*. He goes by DAX like the character in the book and is the only other gay guy Jackson and I have ever met.

"So is your dick head purple?" I asked him when MJ introduced us.

"Ah. You've read the book."

I nodded. "I've read practically all of Harold Robbins."

"What about Jacqueline Susann?" DAX asked.

"Of course. And Kyle Onstott and Lancer Horner—"

"*Mandingo. Falconhurst Fancy. Master of Falconhurst—*"

"*The Tattooed Rood* was one of my favorites."

Jackson looked from one of us to the other, then shrugged. MJ tried not to roll her eyes but failed.

"How did you get your hands on those books?" DAX asked. "They were pretty forbidden."

"I found my grandmother's stash. Until then, I thought she'd only ever taken care of my grandfather and baked. Reading those books, I really wished I'd gotten to know her—to thank her, I mean. Those books taught me everything I know about sex."

DAX stared at me for a minute as if measuring me. "What about *Child of the Sun*?"

"The one where the future emperor of Rome loved men? Oh, man, that book changed everything for me."

"Me, too." He grinned. "So you're…"

"Yeah, we both are," I said indicating Jackson. "We're a couple."

"Did your mother really name you after a character in a novel?" MJ asked, appalled.

"Oh, yeah. When I was seven, she had it legally changed—my name before that was Jorge. By the time I was ten, her hopes that I would be some kind of lady killer, like the original DAX, were dashed." He laughed, a light tinkling sound as bright as his hair.

"You have gray hair," Jackson said suddenly, staring at DAX's tangle of silvery hair.

"Yes," DAX said. He sounded amused. "All the men in my family start turning gray at puberty."

Monday, February 20, 1978, University City—"So, Jackson is a preacher's kid?" MJ asked, chewing her gum furiously.

I looked up from my textbook and nodded.

"Is he, like, super religious? Should I not curse in front of him?"

I laughed. MJ is pretty foul-mouthed. "No, He doesn't really believe in his father's notion of God and religion. Actually, he thinks he's full of shit."

MJ seemed scandalized. "What about you? Do you think his father is full of shit?"

"I do. I think all religious leaders are. I mean, I don't believe in organized religion. It's just a bunch of power-mad men exploiting people's desires and fears. Dante reserves a special Circle in hell for them."

"The Eighth Circle, right?"

I looked at her in surprise. How many people our age have read Dante's *Inferno*? "Yes, Bolgia, two to be exact—"

"Upside down in shit and howling mad."

I didn't want to admit to her how pleasing I find picturing Reverend Jack and his congregation upside down in shit—shit thrown at them by Reverend Jack and his Bible—as they howl and fight amongst themselves, so instead I laughed. "Yes."

"But that was for flatterers. How do preachers fit in?"

"They flatter the faithful by assuring them they are walking in the path of righteousness and then play on their fear that others not following the same path threatens their sanctity with eternal damnation, thus turning people against each other."

MJ popped her gum as she does when she is in deep thought.

"OK, enough talk about religion. We have work to do." We were supposed to be looking at the central tenets of change management theory and using them to create a strategy for a corporate merger scenario our organizational psychology professor had assigned us.

Sunday, March 19, 1978, University City—DAX, awed by Jackson's pervasive but easy masculinity, and after declaring him the last of the great men, has assigned him the title, "his butch hotness," which I think embarrasses Jackson. DAX uses the term much as one would use His Majesty to refer to the King of England: "How was his butch hotness when you left for class this morning?" "Do you and his butch hotness want to go see *The Rocky Horror Picture Show* this weekend?"

I think this masculinity of Jackson's, his ability to "pass," will serve him well, as tomorrow he will start his plumbing apprenticeship. He says the guys he's met are "all right," though a bit aggressive and rowdy. If they notice his reticence to talk about women or his straightforward disinterest in female staff members of their company, they chalk it up to "shyness" and his being a preacher's kid.

He'll apprentice for five years; he'll have to get 2,000 hours of on-the-job training and 224 hours of classroom instruction each of the five years. I'll graduate before he finishes his apprenticeship, but once he's done, he'll have his journeyman plumber's license.

It feels good to be able to plan a future together.

Friday, March 24, 1978, University City—I was reorganizing the director of student living's files when Noel, our student receptionist, stuck his head in the door and said, "Here come the Ning sisters right on schedule."

I sighed and stepped out into the reception area to watch the familiar drama. I busied myself misting the plastic plants—best way to fight dust—and eavesdrop. Jon, from the depths of his chair, muttered, "No, no. I'm not talking to them again."

The "Ning" sisters—I've yet to learn their real names—are freshmen like me. They are Jewish sisters, twins who come in at least thrice weekly to complain. Their complaints range from the slowness of their high-rise dorm's elevators to the absence of name badges on the work-study students who staff the security desk, to the temperature of the hot water in their room. Their biggest complaint is about some unspecified defect in the construction of their dorm that is causing them to be sick; the symptoms of the alleged illness are as vague as its alleged cause.

Months ago, they'd stopped by late on a Friday afternoon, as was their wont, to insist that some action be taken. Frustrated, Noel had dragged out Jon, the director of student living, who was already half shrugged into his coat. I watched him from my position beside the plastic plants. He, with his balding pate, bowed legs and flat behind, tried desperately to find out what was wrong. "We're sick," they insisted repeatedly. Each time they said "sick," I added, perhaps a trifle too loudly, "ning." The name stuck and henceforth they were known as the "Ning" sisters.

Jon and Noel were still in Jon's office furiously whispering. I sidled up to the counter, misting bottle in hand. "Listen," I said addressing the sisters, "I've been here for a while, so I know you've been having symptoms."

They nodded rigorously. *Finally, someone is listening.*

"Well, I'm not sure folks here can help you. But I remember my granny—God rest her soul—always recommended having an enema whenever you were feeling unwell for a period of time. 'Flushes out the system,' she used to say."

The sisters nodded vigorously and, chattering excitedly among themselves, turned to leave. "Thank you," they called out over their shoulders.

"Let me know if it works."

When Noel finally reemerged—*sans* Jon, I noticed—he asked, "Where'd they go?"

I shrugged. "Guess they got tired of waiting."

Tuesday, April 4, 1978, University City—We were working on our presentations for our Gender in Media course, which examines media representations of femininity, masculinity, and orientation, the impact of that messaging on consumers of media, and the role and responsibility media reporters play in shaping public opinion, when MJ said, "I've never met anyone like you. At school, there were girls who were suspect and whispered about—teachers too—but they were all so uncomfortable, it was as if they were wearing wool sweaters in the dead of summer." MJ had attended one of the most exclusive girls' boarding schools on the East Coast.

"That's because they were trying to meet parental expectations and fit into social norms, and by the way, when people say something like heterosexuality is normal, what they really mean is 'common,' but we tend to accept their definition of normal and let that shape us into believing we are abnormal, deviant and as such, *less than* everyone else. That's the thing that struck me immediately about Jackson. He wasn't interested in being what everyone thought he should be—even if he was a preacher's kid. He was defiantly himself. At sixteen, he asked me out on a date—"

"But that's just it. You seem to go beyond defiance. You seem so... comfortable in your skin."

"I have eczema," I said. "I am uncomfortable in my literal skin. I can't imagine being uncomfortable in my metaphorical skin as well."

Friday, April 28, 1978, University City—In my Romance in Fiction class today—I've decided to minor in English Lit—our professor asked us to name great romantic couples. The usual was offered up: Romeo and Juliet; Antony and Cleopatra. When she called on me, perhaps because I was tired from working and classes and studying and loving Jackson, I blurted, "Batman and Robin." There was initial silence, then the not-unexpected twittering and giggling. The professor rapped on her podium.

"I don't understand this reaction. If two people love each other, the fact that they are of the same sex does not negate that love."

I was stunned. I'd never heard anyone make such a statement before. I didn't feel validated, for from the moment I first kissed Jackson, I have been of the school of *If loving you is wrong, I don't want to be right.* But I felt seen, worthy of acknowledgment. If Jackson and I hadn't stumbled into a new world, it was certainly an unimagined territory.

"Batman and Robin weren't gay. They weren't a couple," said one pale, effeminate, long-haired student who I thought of as the "reluctant gay."

"Who's to say they weren't?" I asked.

"You just want them to be gay because you are," he accused.

"You may have a valid point," our professor said, "but don't we all interpret the world and thus literature through lenses formed by our individual beliefs, desires, and perception of the world? Why is Oren's interpretation less valid than yours?"

"*Batman* aired from 1966 to 1968, before 'gay' was a thing—"

"Gay has always been a 'thing,'" I snapped.

"Oren is interpreting this in a post-Stonewall era," the reluctant gay insisted.

"Isn't all art, including literature, viewed through a contemporary lens?" our professor shot back.

I turned to the reluctant gay. "*Batman* the TV show may not have been explicitly gay, but it was certainly informed by a not-so-subtle gay sensibility. Look at the Joker with his face full of pancake makeup and lipstick, and the Riddler flitting around in what was essentially a green catsuit with question marks all over it. What is he doing if not questioning the heteronormative narrative that was meant to be the perceived default for the series?"

I floated through the rest of my classes on a cloud. Tonight, we were lying on the couch when I told Jackson what happened in class. He laughed. "Wait," he said, "Which one of us is Batman? Who's Robin?"

"You'll always be my Batman," I told him. He lay back down, and I settled my head on his stomach. "I'm hungry," I said.

He sat up abruptly. "Alfred," he shouted, "we're hungry. When's dinner?"

Monday, May 8, 1978, University City—Today, crossing the Quad, I ran into the reluctant gay whose name is Jeremy. He pulled me onto a bench and sat beside me. "I'm gay," he said simply.

I struggled with an appropriate response: *How nice for you. Welcome to the club. Oh, I'm shocked. Yes, I know.* I settled on murmuring noncommittally.

"Except," he confided, "I don't like anal sex."

"Oh," I said, promptly filing the information in the part of my brain where I put things I never intend to think about ever again, like the farm, my grandfather, my parents' death.

"Well," he said brightly, "I'm off to student health. I'm pretty sure I have gonorrhea."

I pulled open the dusty file cabinet in my brain once again.

Saturday, October 14, 1978, University City—MJ and I were studying for midterms. She sat at the tiny desk in my and Jackson's bedroom, and I sprawled on the bed. She pulled my parents' wedding album off the shelf above the desk and began looking through it. Again.

She paused at a photo that showed my parents standing in front of a mantel; seated in front of them in a frothy lace dress and a modest hat was my grandmother. "Tell me again. Who's the gentleman next to your dad?"

"That's his father, my grandfather, Grampy Eddie."

"You called him Grampy Eddie?"

"Everyone did," I said. I did not tell her that Grampy Eddie was known as the "king of numbers" back in Springfield. The illegal gambling operation had made him wealthy, which paid for the new Buick every two years and an endless string of girlfriends, not always his alone. For all the kids in the neighborhood, he was an endless source of quarters and penny candies.

MJ turned to a page on which my mother's maid-of-honor was setting the headpiece that held her veil onto her head as they gazed at their joint reflection in an enormous shadowbox mirror. "Your mom was so beautiful," MJ said.

"Yeah, and Dad was handsome. I used to wonder if I'd look like him when I grew up. He used to call me 'little man,'" I suddenly recalled.

"Do you miss them?"

I shrugged. "I don't really remember them."

"You don't have any baggage, do you?" MJ asked.

"Sorry?"

"Emotional baggage, I mean. After all you've been through—losing your parents so young, growing up gay... Did someone used to hit you?"

"What?" I asked, startled, trying not to think of my grandfather, of the bullies at school...

"I'm sorry. It's just that if anyone makes a sudden move towards you—even me—to, like, hug you, you wince. And your whole body stiffens as if you expect a blow."

And just like that, memories I'd thought long forgotten returned. I remembered black eyes and bruised ribs and hands heavy with prayer-like fists raining down.

I sat up and tried to collect my thoughts. From the stereo in the living room, Donna Summer lamented about the melting of a cake left out in the rain and a recipe lost from memory to a throbbing disco beat.

"Sorry," MJ said. "I didn't mean to pry, or embarrass you—"

"You didn't." And she hadn't. I wasn't aware that I did that wincing thing, though I'm not surprised. I guess I *am* surprised that anyone cared enough to notice.

"I just meant to point out that despite what's happened to you, none of it seems to have left you with baggage."

"I travel light," I said. "I carry no baggage that can't be checked curbside or stuffed in an overhead compartment."

"Are you two studying? I hear an awful lot of talking," Jackson yelled from the kitchen, drowning out Donna for a moment. "I'm making a snack, but only studiers can have some."

MJ lingered over the last photo in my parents' wedding album. In it, my parents are looking back at the photographer from the back seat of Grampy Eddie's 1958 Buick Century convertible. My dad's arm rests across my mother's bare shoulders. They are both smiling. Grampy Eddie sits up front behind the steering wheel, his back to the camera; the inevitable fedora set at a rakish angle covers his head. On the trunk of the Buick are the words: *Just Married*. With a sigh, MJ closed the album. As she returned it to its spot on the shelf, she asked, "Do you think you'll ever get married?"

"What? That's ridiculous. No."

Jackson burst in just then carrying a bowl of Jiffy popcorn glistening with butter and salt.

Saturday, October 21, 1978, University City—Saturday afternoons, what I have begun to think of as our "gang of seven" hang out at our apartment—DAX, MJ, Perils, Sue P, Faiz, Jackson, and me. DAX was reclining on our sofa tossing popcorn from the bowl resting on his stomach into his mouth when he asked, "So, what are we doing for Halloween?" When no one responded, he sat up and demanded, "None of you have made plans?"

We—MJ, Perils, Sue P, Faiz, Jackson, and I—shook our heads, no.

"Pathetic," he said. "Fine. I'll make plans. We're going trick-or-treating, then we'll hop the bars downtown."

We looked at each other, but no one dared contradict him, even though I was sure we were all thinking, *aren't we're too old to go trick-or-treating*?

"OK, it's settled," DAX declared. "We're going trick-or-treating together. We'll meet here Tuesday around five-thirty."

Jackson and I looked at each other, wondering when our tiny apartment had become the official launch pad for our gang's little adventures.

"I've always wanted to go trick-or-treating," I offered.

"You've never been trick-or-treating?" DAX asked incredulously. The others just stared at me in mute astonishment.

"No, and neither has Jackson." They all turned to stare at Jackson.

"It's true," Jackson said. "Neither of us have been."

"How is that possible?" MJ wondered aloud.

Easy. When I'd asked to be taken trick-or-treating back in Springfield, Grampy Eddie had nixed the idea with a firm *no*, adding, "We are not poor. There is no need for you to dress up as a fool and go begging the neighbors for candy."

And of course, in Locust Hollow there was *no* Halloween, Reverend Jack having decreed it an opportunity to pay homage to the devil, but more dangerously, through costuming and wandering the darkened streets, you were inviting the devil himself into your home and offering him a seat in your favorite chair.

"Is Halloween a big holiday here?" Jackson asked.

"Only for children and the gays," Perils said.

"Chil'," DAX said, "Halloween is gay Christmas."

"Gay Christmas?"

"Yes. Well, now, anyway. During the fifties and sixties, Halloween was known as 'bitches Christmas.' All the gays dressed up in drag and bar hopped. It was really special because normally it was illegal to cross dress, but on Halloween, folks could get away with dressing in drag—for a lot of folks, it was the only time they could appear in public as their true selves. So that's why Halloween is so important to us gays."

Tuesday, October 31, 1978, University City—Perils arrived dressed as Cat Woman from *Batman* and carried her family's remarkably placid calico cat in her arms. When anyone commented on how cute the cat was, she would insist it was a dog in a cat costume. Most people laughed, while others stepped back in wary confusion. MJ was the Tin Man from *The Wizard of Oz*. She'd painted one of her perpetual overalls silver, placed an aluminum watering can on her head, and Perils had helped her paint her face and hands with a silver body paint they'd found at Spencer's Gifts. Jackson took one look at her and, calling her contagious, told her not to sit on any furniture. "Don't even lean against the walls," he admonished.

Faiz was dressed as Tony Manero from *Saturday Night Fever* in a white three-piece suit, black shirt with a wide collar, and platform shoes; Sue P was dressed as a "disco lady" in a two-piece bedazzled black-and-white jumpsuit with a matching headband.

Jackson and I were dressed up as Butch Cassidy and the Sundance Kid. MJ looked us over from her station in the middle of our living room and nodded approvingly.

When DAX showed up looking like his normal self, Perils demanded to know where his costume was. "I'm wearing it," he said.

"Oh? And who are you supposed to be?"

He waited a beat then, tossing his silvery head and placing his hands on his hips—thumbs *forward*—he lisped, "A young American homosexual."

LARRY BENJAMIN

"Well done," Perils said before declaring him the winner of
the best costume contest that had until that moment existed
exclusively in her head. She handed him his prize: a victor's box
of eclairs.

"Shall we go?" DAX asked.

We dispersed into the neighborhood immediately surrounding
campus, joining costumed actual children, their harried-looking
parents, and their trailing, picture-snapping grandparents. If
anyone thought we were too old to be trick-or-treating, they
certainly didn't say anything, cheerfully inviting us to dive into
proffered bowls of candy. We walked until our bags of candy
became burdensome to carry. Next, we hopped the trolley into
town and went bar hopping in the gayborhood, where we actually
seemed like children compared to the costumed, bejeweled
revelers—devils and witches, drag queens of every size and
description, a Michelin man.

After, at home, stripped of his costume, Jackson fell onto the bed
and said, "Man, what a night."

Indeed. I looked around and didn't see the devil seated anywhere
in our apartment.

BLUE (1979)

Thursday, February 15, 1979, University City—It was not quite midnight when we heard someone knocking on the front door. The knocking stopped for a few minutes, like a held breath, then started up again as I drifted back into sleep. The knocking became steady, insistent. Jackson, faster to rise than I and better at gathering his wits on waking, threw back the covers and headed into the living room. As I crawled out of bed, I could hear two voices, strident though whispering. I arrived in the living room to find Sue P standing with Jackson in heated conversation.

"What's going on? I asked, yawning. "Sue P, what are you doing here?"

Jackson turned to me, his exasperation evident. "She's looking for MJ. For some reason, she thinks she's here."

"Is MJ here?" Sue P asked me.

"What? No. Why would you think she'd be here?"

"You're always together."

Before I could respond, she sat on the sofa: to say she crumbled onto the sofa would be a more accurate description.

"What's wrong, Sue?"

"Nothing. MJ's mother called a little while ago wanting to talk to her, and I have no idea where she is, so I just thought she'd be here. Do you know where she is?"

"Actually, I don't." I didn't want to point out that it was Valentine's Day.

"Oh, dear. Oh, dear!"

"Where's Faiz," I asked, looking around.

"In his dorm room, sleeping, I imagine." She looked at me in exasperation. "Why does everyone act like Faiz and I are always together?"

"Because ya are, Blanche, ya are always together," Jackson drawled in his dead-on imitation of Bette Davis. I tried to think of a time when I'd seen one of them without the other; couldn't.

"Do you really think MJ is OK?"

"I do."

"OK. I should probably get back home. Night."

This morning, when MJ slipped into her usual seat beside me in the lecture hall, I glanced at her. She didn't look any the worse for wear, so I said, "So, you *weren't* abducted by aliens?"

"Oh, yeah, that," MJ said.

"Good Valentine's Day?"

"Yeah." One word, said with finality. Then, softening her tone, she added, "Sorry Sue P woke you guys—"

"It's fine. Everything OK?"

"Yeah, I called my mother this morning."

"This *morning*?" I raised my eyebrows. She ignored me, suddenly finding the class syllabus riveting.

"Did she ask where you were?"

"Yeah, of course," she said. Then she added nonchalantly, "I told her I spent the night with you."

"You told her you were with me?"

"Well, yeah. I couldn't tell her where I actually spent the night."

"What did she say?"

"She asked if we were serious."

"About what?"

"Us, silly."

"Us?"

"Oh…"

"Apparently, I talk about you so much, she thought we were dating—oh, don't look so horrified. There are worse things than dating a girl."

Name one, I wanted to say but bit my tongue.

"So, what did you tell her?"

"I told her it wasn't like that. I told her you're gay."

Oh, and?"

"And now she wants to meet you. You and Jackson are invited over for a swim and Easter dinner. You must come, otherwise she will think I lied about being with you and assume that means I'm the whore of Babylon. Or something."

"Wait," I said, "You have a *pool*?"

She shot me a look. I retreated.

"So—if you weren't with me—and we know you weren't—where were you?"

"Professor's here," she said, pointing. "And you know how testy she gets when people talk in class instead of scrambling to gather the pearls of wisdom she's dropping."

MJ is poetic sometimes and notoriously evasive about her love life always. She insists that because she wants to be a reporter and an anchorwoman, people need to be more interested in what she has to report than in what she does.

Sunday, April 15, 1979, University City—MJ's father is a lawyer; her mother is an interior designer, so I suppose I shouldn't have been surprised that their house is stunning. They live in a stately brick Georgian surrounded by towering pines and enormous shade trees—Japanese maple, weeping willows, dogwoods. A terraced flagstone patio in the back steps down to the deck of a pool filled with beckoning blue water. Jackson and I hadn't been swimming since we left Locust Hollow. Jackson, MJ, and I swam and played half-hearted water volleyball ball while Mr. and Mrs. Mitchell lay on exquisite chaise longues drinking cocktails and talking quietly.

Before dinner, MJ led us back to the pool house so we could shower and change for dinner. Their pool house is bigger than our apartment.

MJ's mother seemed positively giddy to have two gay guys in her house, seated at her table, which was a forest of floral-patterned Wedgewood China attended by a battalion of Waterford crystal, set ablaze by candlelight. There were candles on the table in front of us, in the light fixture above our heads, and in the sconces over the fireplace. The walls were covered in an opulent, hand-painted silk de Gournay wallpaper featuring a landscape filled with toucans, lovebirds, parrots, and macaws alongside jewel-toned serpents, ornate butterflies, and swinging monkeys on a light-blue background.

Throughout dinner, hidden speakers released country music as soft and impossible to grasp as fragrance or a London fog. As MJ's father poured us wine, Crystal Gayle confided over strings about something or other that made her brown eyes blue.

After dinner, we had coffee and cognac by the pool.

As we drove home in MJ's hideous burnt-orange Volvo, she confided, "Claude adores you guys."

"Oh, good," I mumbled. Jackson was asleep in the backseat, and I was drifting off in the passenger seat, no doubt from the unaccustomed effects of the cognac. I sat up. Rubbing my eyes, I said, "Wait, who's Claude?"

"My mother."

"Your mother's name is Claude?"

"Yes. My grandmother had several miscarriages—all girls—before my mother was born. Apparently, there is an old wives' tale that dictates if you have 'trouble keeping a girl,' you should give your first surviving daughter a boy's name."

"Oh."

MJ glanced over at me. "Go back to sleep," she said. "I'll wake you when we get to your place."

As we were brushing our teeth, I asked Jackson, "Did you have a good time tonight?"

He spat in the sink and said, "I did. But it was kind of strange. Up until tonight, I didn't realize a world like that existed."

87

I understood; until tonight, I hadn't either. Hearing the wonder in his voice, I vowed to myself that we would come to know that world more intimately, *that we would be a part of that world.*

Thursday, April 26, 1979, University City—I had lunch with MJ today at the cafeteria for students who lived on campus and signed up for a meal plan. The first time I'd accompanied MJ here for lunch, I'd been overwhelmed by the sheer amount and variety of food on display. I got dizzy waiting in line, watching the ladies in hairnets eager to serve, spoons ready, behind heat lamps that glowed red-orange-red like billboards advertising vacation packages to hell, offering culinary temptations for every taste bud, the desserts and ice creams lying provocatively on their beds of ice...

"Dude, are you OK?" MJ asked, nudging me as I stared dumbfounded at the lavish display.

I nodded. "I'm fine. Why?"

"You look like you've never seen food before."

Of course, I had seen food before—but never in such abundance. Back in Locust Hollow, folks would share what they had for meals, but the truth was no one had much. Our planned dinner party is this weekend.

As we exited through a turnstile, I turned to shush MJ while stifling my larcenous giggles as the flatware and crockery MJ had nicked banged together in her purse. My own pilfered goods were quieter and better behaved in my knapsack.

I felt guilty and wondered how I could return the stolen goods after our dinner party. MJ did not share my sense of guilt. She saw herself as a kind of Robin Hood, redistributing the assets of the wealthy into the hands of the poor, in this case taking from the university and giving to poor college students. But I was less sure. Surely, our theft would result in higher tuition, which is what universities call their system of taxation. Thus, I think she was more like a member of Congress, cutting taxes on the rich and making the poor and middle-classes pay for it. But I kept my thoughts to myself and loved her no less.

As we were making our getaway, we ran into Perils, whose actual name is Pauline. Perils works behind the chocolate counter and as a bartender at her family's after-dinner lounge, which specializes in handmade chocolate, unique desserts, and "craft" cocktails. Because she is always relating some drama that occurred over chocolate martinis and candy sales, I'd nicknamed her The Perils of Praline—so many customers with nut allergies had gone into anaphylactic shock after eating her family's classic pralines despite multiple posted warnings about them containing nuts, and the paramedics called so often they had finally stopped offering them, substituting a pure chocolate version. The name stuck but was shortened to Perils. She is good-natured about her nickname, though, and serves as our resident bartender at our tender soirees, since she is the only one old enough to procure alcohol. She introduced our little group into the world of adult cocktails—Black Russians, Universes, Moscow Mules—and moderation at a time when our peers were getting drunk, and throwing up Olde English 800, Rolling Rock, and grain alcohol.

MJ shifted her handbag on her shoulder, which was starting to droop from the weight of her ill-gotten gains. Flatware giggled and crockery clapped.

"What *is* that sound?" Perils asked, cocking her head.

"What sound?" we asked in unison, the very embodiment of innocence.

"So, listen," Perils went on, ignoring us and popping her gum. "Saturday, we hosted a wedding breakfast at the restaurant. Fifty people. The bride and groom had their own table in the middle of the room raised up on a little dais they had us build. It was very strange. Something was clearly amiss, but I wasn't getting disaster vibes—until the bride and groom were served their brunch order. I brought out their order…"

I wasn't surprised by Perils' leading role; Perils always plays a leading role in the perilous situations at the restaurant.

"…Chocolate Belgian waffles with ricotta, orange marmalade topped with shaved chocolate and orange zest. The best man takes one look at it on the table and screams at the groom, 'How could you share our special breakfast with *her*?' He bursts into tears, and the groom says, "I didn't know she was ordering it!' By now, everyone knows what is amiss. I hear there's going to be an annulment coming. I heard this morning that the groom and best man are in Aruba on what was supposed to be the groom's honeymoon. I guess boyfriend figures if she tried to steal his man, he can steal her honeymoon."

Perils, cheerfully ignoring our stunned silence, chirped, "Anyway, loves, I must dash. I'll see you at the dinner party on Saturday. I'm bringing the booze."

MJ shifted her handbag on her shoulder and waved, causing a renewed clatter. Perils cocked her head, and mumbled again, "What *is* that sound?"

Saturday, April 28, 1979, University City—"Wow your apartment is so orderly and clean," Sue P commented when they arrived this afternoon. "Is it always like this?"

"Always," MJ put in.

"My dad," I said, "taught me to keep things clean."

"I still find it odd that your father essentially taught you how to keep house," MJ said.

"Rather than my mother, you mean?"

"Well, that he taught you at all. If you were to learn those things, I would have thought your mother would have been the one."

"I told you, my father learned all that at the children's home." The truth was my mother was more likely to paint a fresco on the dining room ceiling than scrub a toilet. I've always thought that if we'd stayed in Springfield, if she had gone to art school like she wanted, she would have eventually had a career as an artist.

"Aren't you being a bit sexist here, MJ?" Sue P asked, effectively ending the conversation. We set to work preparing for our dinner party.

Sue P, MJ, and I started to cook together in our tiny galley kitchen. We made sausage and peppers—with sausage from the terminal market downtown that reminded Jackson and I of the sausage the farmers in Locust Hollow made and sold, and burgers and home fries. As we cooked, Jackson set out the plates and forks and knives.

"I hope we have enough," MJ fretted.

Ever practical, Sue P said, "Next time, let's just have folks bring their own plates and utensils."

We ended up with ten or twelve people. People sat on what furniture we had and on the floor with plates in their laps. Someone brought a jug of Boone's Farm apple wine; Perils sneered at it but gamely had a glass with dinner.

We were having dessert when Faiz, tipsy, started to cry. This was so far from his usual bubbly personality everyone was immediately alarmed. Everyone loves Faiz. He is sweet. With eccentric Middle Eastern looks and a mass of curly black hair, he is always smiling. He and Sue P dote on each other; they go everywhere together, causing endless speculation about whether they are a couple: *are they, or aren't they?* They often contradict each other on this point.

"Faiz!"

"Faiz, what's wrong?"

"I may have breast cancer."

"What?"

"You do not have breast cancer," Sue P objected. Sue P is the most maternal of our friends, but she has no patience with drama that she sees as nonsense.

"You don't know that. I have a tumor in my breast—"

"Chest," Sue P corrected.

Faiz glared at her through his tears. "I'm having surgery on Monday."

"Oh, Faiz…"

"Do you want one of us to go with you?"

"No. Sue P is going with me."

Sue P. Evidently there had been two Sues at some point, so the first initial of Sue P's last name had been added to her first name to distinguish between the two. No one could remember a second Sue, though. Nonetheless, the moniker persisted.

The fuss and attention soothed Faiz, and he was soon laughing again. We moved to the courtyard for cookies and milk, which Perils insisted would absorb the alcohol we had consumed and prevent hangovers.

Monday, April 30, 1979, University City—Today was a quintessential spring morning, warm and bright, not a cloud in the sky. Still high on the success of our first dinner party, I fairly skipped along after my first class on my way to Dodo for a snack and coffee. I saw Sue P and Faiz leaving the university hospital. When they reached my side of the street, I asked, "So how did it go?"

"Fine," Faiz chirped. "They removed the tumor. They're pretty sure it was benign."

"It was just a fatty tumor," Sue P said.

"They were worried about scarring," Faiz said. "So they had a plastic surgeon suture the incision."

"Really?"

"Yeah. Wanna see?"

Before I could stop him, he pulled his T-shirt over his head. "Shit," he said. "That hurt."

"The doctor told you to avoid lifting your arm over your head for a few days."

"Oh, right. See?" he said stretching towards me. I peered at his chest just above his nipple, where there was a small Band-Aid.

I looked at Sue P, who just rolled her eyes.

"Well, I'm so glad everything turned out OK. Listen, I have to grab something to eat then head to my next class—and you probably need to go lay down or something to recover."

"Yeah, yeah. We'll talk later. Let everyone know I pulled through."

"Will do," I called, hiding my smile as Sue P led him towards his dorm.

Saturday, September 22, 1979, University City—I heard Jackson open our apartment's door then exclaim, "You, again?"

"Oh, hush," I heard MJ say. "You've barely seen me. I was gone all summer. Besides, you know I'm here because I adore you both. And I know you love me, Jackson. Also, I hate messiness—Sue P is a slob—and your place is always so clean and orderly, even though you're both guys—"

"Whoa, girlfriend," Jackson said in that queeny voice he sometimes adopts—his ability to code switch, that is change his presentation from uber masculine to effeminate gay at will, still startles me every time he does it. "You need to check your assumptions about gender. Also, I am a preacher's kid, and cleanliness is next to godliness."

Jackson was, I knew, serious. Despite working as a plumber, I've never seen Jackson dirty. Each morning, he leaves our apartment dressed in neat khakis and a carefully pressed button-down shirt. He returns home dressed as he left. On Fridays, he comes home with a brown paper bag under his arm, which contains his soiled work clothes. Even after a long day that includes overtime, he returns to me smelling of soap and aftershave. That is one of the things I love about him—that he always chooses to show me the best version of himself.

"Pardon my mistake, good sir," MJ said bowing. "Oren," she shouted when she saw me standing in the hall watching them, "Thank God you're here. Please save me from this psychopath you're in love with."

I laughed, helplessly charmed by their manic antics in opposition to each other.

Saturday, October 20, 1979, University City—I was writing a paper for my comparative literature class. Tomorrow, I will go over to MJ's room and type it on her fancy electric typewriter. I generally type her papers for her as well, as she is a terrible typist—think seven or eight words a minute, *with typos*. As MJ moons over my proficiency, in my head, I thank Mrs. Campbell, my typing teacher, who ignored the consternation of all the other teachers and the school's principal over my decision to take typing rather than shop and welcomed me into her distaff den.

On the radio, Prince was insisting he wanted to be our brother, and our mother and our sister, too. Jackson came up behind me and wrapped his arms around me. "This song is for us."

"What do you mean?"

"We're everything to each other. And all we have."

I twisted in my chair to look at him. "Does that make you sad?" I asked.

"No." He giggled and whispered in my ear, "I want to be your lover, too."

"You *are* my lover, silly boy." I pulled him onto my lap.

He made himself comfortable and looked into my eyes. He looks at me and I feel like a hero. Yet I know it is he who saved me.

"I love you, Blue Moon," I said.

"I know," he answered kissing me. "I love you, too."

He pulled me to my feet, and we tumbled onto the bed. After, he looked pensive. "What's wrong?" I asked him.

"I heard from Reverend Jack today."

"What did he have to say?"

"The usual. He thinks this will get us sent to hell." He held our entwined fingers in the air. "Do you think it will?"

I rolled onto my stomach. "You know on Judgment Day, when St. Peter stops me at the pearly gates and asks me what I did with my life, I will tell him I spent it loving you."

"You think that will be enough to get you into heaven?"

I shrugged. "Living with you, loving you in the open, is my heaven. Nothing else matters." I kissed him, laid my head down on my pillow. He slapped me on my naked ass. "No sleeping. Get up. You have a paper to write."

"No," I said, rolling onto my back. "Come here. I can write it in the morning."

INDIGO (1980)

Saturday, April 5, 1980, University City—Today is the fourth anniversary of our first date. To celebrate, we went to a matinee to see a revival of the musical, *Your Arm's too Short to Box with God*, a phrase which Jackson, being a preacher's kid, was quite familiar with and thus excited to see the play. Afterwards, we went to Indigo, a popular restaurant in the gayborhood. Inside, it was cool and dark. The walls were painted a flat indigo under swirls of glossy violet and blue. The doors and banquettes were upholstered in tufted purple velvet. As our eyes adjusted to the dark, an ethereal young man, dressed all in blue, glided out of the shadows.

"Good evening," he said softly. "Welcome to Indigo. The color indigo sits between blue and violet in the rainbow, and like the color itself, the Indigo experience represents tranquility, harmony, confidence, and integrity. Are you here for Four-twenty or Four-forty?"

"I beg your pardon?" Jackson said.

"Are you here for," he sounded slightly bored and disappointed, "Four-twenty, the restaurant, or Four-forty, the dance club upstairs."

"Oh," Jackson said. "The restaurant."

"Excellent," the ghost said and, grabbing two menus, added, "Follow me."

"Oh, I get it," I said, suddenly remembering a science lesson on rainbows. "Indigo is visible in the light spectrum at a wavelength of four-twenty to four-forty nanometers."

The ghost stopped so abruptly Jackson walked into him. He shot Jackson an annoyed look, then, addressing me, said, "No one ever gets that."

A waiter, also dressed in blue, so harmonized with the décor that he appeared to materialize out of thin air, brought us water and detailed the evening's specials. Everyone there appeared to move on silent cat feet, quiet and stealth and without disturbing the tranquil air.

Our waiter asked if we were celebrating a special occasion. Jackson told him it was our fourth anniversary as he reached for my hand. This is still so new to us—being able to be openly affectionate in public. Watching our clasped hands, the waiter, whose name he insisted was Henri even though he was the least French-looking person I've ever seen, recommended we start with oysters on the half shell, with fermented shallot, York imperial apple mignonette, and Daikon radish. For dinner, Jackson ordered the grilled Iberian pork chop, forest mushrooms, lentil, balsamic braised onion, and horseradish gremolata, and I ordered the glazed duck breast with castelfranco, coffee, black grape, celery root, and vin cotto. I'd never eaten duck before. Just before our meal arrived, the host coalesced from the slight breeze the server left in his wake. He offered us a bottle of Domaine de l'Eveche Pinot Noir, which he insisted was "on the house." He poured it into our glasses then evaporated like a wisp of smoke.

The wine was as rich and dark as the restaurant; we toasted each other and felt very grown up, very much in love, and very far away from Locust Hollow.

Sunday, June 29, 1980, University City—"You've never been to a Pride march?" DAX asked us incredulously last Saturday, as he pawed through a rack of shiny shirts at Lambda Rising—the gay bookstore and thrift shop—in search of something to wear to said march.

"Do you know where we grew up?"

"Well, you going to this one."

"But it's downtown, isn't it?" Jackson asked.

"Yeah. So?"

"So how are we gonna get there? Traffic will be insane, and I read there's a lot of street closures. We can't possibly drive."

"We'll take the trolley, like everyone else," DAX said.

And that's how we found ourselves at our first Gay Pride march today, which was less a march than a strut, a boogie, a twisting joyous dance down the broadest avenue in the city: gayboys, lithe and shirtless, covered in rainbow flags and glitter, shimmied; sequined, towering drag queens on floats tossed beads the colors of a rainbow into the raucous crowd; dykes on bikes, topless, their pasties shimmering in the summer breezes, defiant and scowling, roared past on Harleys and Kawasakis, powerful and loud as tanks on a battlefield.

Silent, clinging to the edges of the crowd were scores of men in hats, whose brims were pulled low over their foreheads, with turned-up collars and glasses so dark it was a wonder they could see. "Bunch of closet queens," DAX pronounced dismissively as Jackson and I rushed along in his dancing wake.

Early in the afternoon, DAX caught a stranger's eye, told us he'd catch up to us later and was gone. I was baffled. In a single glance, he and a stranger had met, recognized each other, and agreed to meet up, across a crowd, without uttering a single word.

Jackson and I wandered aimlessly, taking it all in. The crowd grew, and Jackson took my hand as if afraid I, too, would suddenly disappear.

"What are you thinking?" I asked Jackson as we watched a bunch of men and women dancing together to thunderous disco music on a swaying stage at the end of the street.

"It never occurred to me there could be so *many...of...us.*"

DAX, reappearing as suddenly as he'd vanished, ushered us into a dimly lit bar that was gearing up for the after-march dance party. Giggles, powered by a river of alcohol, burst in the smoky air. Shrieks of "Girlfriend!" and "Miss Thang!" exploded in the room like fireworks. Above the empty dance floor, a mirrored disco ball started to turn faster as the DJ pumped up the volume of the music and began spinning records like a dervish.

Once again, trailing in DAX's brilliant wake, we found ourselves aboard the last trolley to University City. As the trolley hurtled out of the station, I felt like Cinderella being pursued by midnight. As the train sped along its tracks, downtown receded, but its bright lights refused to dim.

Tuesday, November 4, 1980, University City—Today, Jackson, MJ, DAX, Faiz, Sue P, and I all voted for the first time. Perils, who being older has voted before, put herself in charge of leading us to the campus polling place located in the great hall of the church on Locust Walk. She coached us last night on how to operate the voting machines. As each of us emerged from the booth having cast our first vote and feeling very grown up, she led the other voters in line and the poll workers in applause and shouted congratulations. A photographer from the campus newspaper asked us to pose for a group photo. Jimmy Carter was, of course, our man. We were confident he would win, not just because we had used our voices and cast votes in his favor, but really how could he lose to Ronald Reagan—a once-upon-a-time movie star and former president of the Screen Actors Guild and a former two-time governor of California, who was also a failed two-time presidential candidate and who was currently running on a platform to increase federal revenue by lowering taxes, a plan one of his Republican opponents publicly derided as "voodoo economics," aided by his plastic, Barbie doll wife, former starlet and current lady in red, Nancy?

Wednesday, November 5, 1980, University City—We woke up to the devastating news that Carter lost to Reagan. I heard the news when my alarm clock went off. I immediately changed the station only to hear the same grim words. I padded into the living room and turned on our small black-and-white TV. It was true: Ronald Reagan had beaten the president. I turned the TV off and went into the kitchen where I found Jackson crying over his cereal bowl. I've never seen him cry before. I gently took the bowl from him and wrapped my arms around him. "It'll be OK," I said, "We'll win next time." With a conviction I did not feel, I added, "A pendulum will only swing so far in one direction before it inevitably swings in the opposite direction."

I can't help but feel that our first exercise in responsible citizenry resulted in absolute failure. All across campus, dejected students are staggering about, still wearing their "Carter/Mondale 1980" buttons.

VIOLET (1981)

Monday, May 11, 1981, University City—Graduation was yesterday. It's hard to believe four years have passed since Jackson and I struck out on our own.

I saw the "Ning" sisters—they looked radiant and healthy. They, like nearly every other graduate, were surrounded by their beaming parents and a bevy of older people I assumed were grandparents. Jackson was the only one in my corner, cheering as I received my diploma. He and I went out to lunch to celebrate. Then we went to MJ's parents for a proper family celebration, as her mother termed it when she called to invite us.

MJ opened the door, looking spectacular in a violet sheathe dress with exaggerated shoulders that hugged curves her perpetual coveralls had hidden. Her subtle makeup—again, a new addition—highlighted her prettiness without softening the strength of her character; her pale-pink lipstick accentuated her full mouth so capable of speaking hard truths and breaking bad news compassionately. *She'll be an excellent anchorwoman someday*, I thought.

Jackson recovered first. "Well, look at you," he said. "Looking like a real girl. And where were you hiding those?" he asked finally, pointing at her cleavage. She slapped his hand away.

Over the last four years, I have watched their relationship morph from acquaintances to that of siblings who delight in needling each other. She was the big, sophisticated sister, he the annoying younger brother determined to remind her he knew her before she was a sophisticate and that they were bound to each other, a *family*—because they both loved me.

Later, when we were alone, I told her how great she looked—not that she looked bad before, but she was different somehow.

"It's because I'm finally comfortable with myself," she said. "And that's because of you."

I asked how that was.

"Freshman year, I remember admiring how comfortable you were in your skin—with being gay and in love with Jackson. You told me you had eczema and were uncomfortable in your literal skin, so you couldn't be uncomfortable in your metaphorical skin as well. Do you remember telling me that?"

"Kind of, I think," I said.

"That really resonated with me because I'd been uncomfortable in my own skin—"

"How so?"

She sighed. "I was fine till puberty hit—a little tomboy, my father's companion. I guess I was the son he never had. Then puberty hit. I grew breasts, only they kept growing. By high school, they were enormous. My back hurt all the time. My shoulders were literally raw from where my bra straps cut into my skin. But the worst of it was the way people treated me. Boys pointed and giggled and seemed to think that my breasts were an invitation for them to try to flirt with me. The girls assumed the size of my breasts made me a slut. So finally, I convinced my parents to let me have breast reduction surgery the summer before we started college. One of the reasons I wore coveralls was to hide the surgical bra I had to wear for months and to protect my breasts from accidental touch—they were incredibly sensitive post-surgery."

"Oh, MJ, I had no idea..."

"I thought everything would be better after surgery, but then I found everyone ignored me—well, mostly boys. I went from too much attention to none at all. But then I met you..."

"Wait. You had to convince your parents to let you have the surgery?"

"Yes. There were concerns. Because of the scar tissue that forms, there was the distinct possibility that I wouldn't be able to breastfeed."

"Oh."

"Yeah. Well, as it turns out, it was a pointless fear. You see, I am as barren as earth that has been burned and salted," MJ explained ruthlessly. Her confession caught me off guard, but I wasn't fooled by her callousness; beneath her words, I could hear hurt and disappointment. I remembered sophomore year, she was always going home to consult with a gynecologist, but I'd assumed this was normal for young women her age. I was surprised and to a degree flattered that she chose to confide in me. I wanted to comfort her but realized this would ruin her trust in me; like me, she doesn't do vulnerable.

Before I could decide on a response, MJ said, "I feel like a failure as a woman. Even a tree grew in Brooklyn. Nothing will ever grow in me."

A Tree Grows in Brooklyn, with its often-hungry protagonist, and Kristin Hunter Lattany's *God Bless the Child*—both books I'd had to borrow from the library the next town over from the farm because I hadn't the means or ability to buy them for myself—did the most to form my character and my determination to go to college, to achieve, to leave generational poverty behind.

Now, I said, "Oh, honey. First of all, you're not a failure as a woman, or as a human being. You're beautiful and smart and kind. It pains me that you think your worth is based on the viability of your womb. You're so much more than an incubator for new life."

She hugged me then. Her breasts pressed against me; I resisted the urge to pull away. *Is this,* I wondered, *what being an adult means? Are these the kinds of conversations adults have?* I felt my childhood slip irretrievably from my grasp.

"Can you go round everyone up?" MJ said. "I have to go touch up my makeup." It was only then I realized she'd been crying. "I want to take a photo of all of us together and have a toast before the fireworks begin. We've been a tribe for four years, and who knows when we'll all be together again."

It was then that I remembered our gang of seven was about to disburse: MJ has landed a job as a reporter with a news station in Virginia; DAX has joined the Peace Corps, of all things; Faiz is headed home for the summer and then on to Oxford in the fall; Sue P is going home to North Dakota, presumably to mourn the loss of Faiz's near-constant presence; Perils is going to the Wharton School of Business for her MBA; and Jackson and I are moving into Center City to begin our lives again.

I stepped through the living room's French doors onto the patio and found Jackson standing holding a drink. The drink told me he was nervous. I took the glass from his hands and drank from it: rum and Coke. I surveyed the scene: there were a couple of dogs and laughing children splashing about in the pool, which was littered with flotation devices, and a handful of smiling adults indulging their antics and allowing themselves to be dunked and splashed with water. All in all, there were throngs of people—around the pool, in the house behind us, spilling onto the lawns—aunts and uncles and cousins and neighbors and friends and MJ's roommates from boarding school. I looked in wonder at all of these people who had come together expressly to celebrate MJ. Jackson, standing beside me, instinctively wrapped his arm around my waist and, leaning his head on my shoulder, murmured, "I know, right?"

MJ re-emerged and joined us—by then, we'd managed to round up our gang of seven. Together, we surveyed the party in the fading light as MJ handed us glasses of Champagne. She paused for a moment, studying each of us in turn, then, raising her glass, said, "To the future."

"To the future," we all agreed, clinking glasses as the first fireworks lit up the sky. The first set spelled out the year: 1981.

Saturday, June 13, 1981, University City—MJ left today to begin her new post-graduation life in Virginia. Jackson and I helped Claude pack up Thing—MJ's reliable but ugly Volvo. Neither MJ nor her father were any help. MJ alternated fighting tears and giving in to her emotions and hugging each of us repeatedly as we struggled with boxes and clothing bags. Her father remained committed to his grief and sat sobbing in the middle of the driveway until Claude dragged him to his feet and away so MJ, who had regained control of herself, could back down the driveway.

As MJ waved and drove away, I realized I would miss Thing. She'd driven us in Thing countless times to have dinner with her parents and to the *Rusty Scupper* to celebrate special occasions like birthdays or acing our finals; and to Chinatown for a Friday night meal after Jackson got paid overtime. These excursions typically ended with me standing in the passenger seat and sticking my head through the open sunroof to sing—poorly but vigorously—along with whatever was playing on the radio, usually Donna Summer or Prince or Rick James.

Inevitably, my sober, sensible preacher's kid would pull me back inside and close the sunroof while MJ and I hissed and booed and called him a spoilsport. "I love you," he'd respond in his reasonable way. "I need to keep you safe because I couldn't bear to lose you. Who would love me if you weren't here?" he would go on to ask. I would surrender myself to the intoxicating effects of alcohol and Jackson's love. I'd reach for his hand over the seat as MJ watched us in the rearview mirror. I'd wake to him carrying me in the front door of our apartment. "I love you," I'd mumble.

"I know you do," he'd respond, nuzzling my neck as he struggled to juggle my weight while inserting his key in the lock.

Once MJ's car had disappeared from sight, we hugged Claude and Octavio.

"We hope you guys will still come to Sunday dinner. Jackson, you can finally join us playing Scrabble," Claude said, practically yelling to be heard over Octavio's sobbing.

"Yes," Jackson replied with badly feigned enthusiasm.

On the Sunday once a month when the three of us went to their house for dinner, we four played Scrabble before dinner while Jackson busied himself fixing a dripping faucet here or unclogging a sink there or clearing the gutters—all things Octavio assured him they could hire someone to do, exhorting him to "Sit down. Relax. Have a beer."

Saturday, August 1, 1981, University City—Jackson and I packed our belongings into the back of his truck and looked up at the Victorian rowhouse with its elaborate trim with its crackling paint that has been our home since we moved to University City. We spent the last four years in a world of scholarships, student loan applications, and bright promise. Today, we are trading that world in for one that repays those student loans, justifies the scholarships, and delivers on that bright promise. I'll have Jackson with me, but I will and already do miss MJ. Long-distance calls are expensive, reserved for deaths and birthdays and Christmas. We promised to write each other weekly, long missives detailing every aspect of our lives that would replace our daily conversations and keep our closeness from diminishing.

"You ready?" Jackson asked, adjusting the rope that held the painting that he had given me as a graduation present, wrapped in brown paper. It was a rendering of the house we have lived in for the last four years. Except for a dagger of late-afternoon sunlight illuminating the wide stoop and the crumbling trim, delicate as fretwork above the broad front door, the painting was dark, brooding as a Rembrandt. In the foreground looking up at the house, Jackson and I stand side by side. You can almost see the hope in our postures.

Jackson and I had grown up separately watching *I Dream of Jeannie* and *Bewitched*; those worlds they showed had been foreign to us, our world being one without joy or magic—until the day Jackson had found me, sitting alone in the bleachers watching Rio playing basketball, and our most fervent wish had been granted.

The resident advisor from campus housing had taken the original photo as he waited for us to come look at the apartment. After we'd signed the lease, he gave us the framed photo as a housewarming present. Jackson had one of the art students turn the photo into a painting. I loved it.

"I'm ready," I said, surprised to see him walk around to the passenger door.

"I'm driving?" I asked.

"Yeah," he said as I slipped behind the wheel. He is so proud of teaching me to drive.

I'm looking forward to our move and starting my new job as a communications specialist with a consulting firm. Jackson will be starting a new plumbing job on a new high-rise office building currently under construction as he continues his apprenticeship. He will be replacing a former colleague who showed up for work three days in a row, as Jackson put it, "higher than a giraffe's ass."

BOOK TWO: 2014–2019

BLACK (2014)

Saturday, March 15, 2014, Center City—Ever since I sold my communications consulting firm last year, Jackson and I have been looking at houses outside the city. We feel like we've outgrown our condo, and certainly the city no longer holds the allure, the promise it once did. Perhaps we've simply "aged out"; the noise, the unfettered youth running through the streets at the weekends has grown tiring. When I proposed leaving the city, Jackson smiled benevolently and, quoting Ruth to Naomi, said, "Wither thou goest, I will go."

I thought of this today as we looked up at *the house*. Built in the late-nineteenth century, it is designed in the French Second Empire Mansard style. It is all cheerful redbrick and cut stone without and black walnut and quarter-sawn oak within. With its decorative slate mansard roof, it exudes a sense of permanence. It is an elaborate wedding cake of a house.

Three stories tall, it is L-shaped with a central tower and a second tower placed at the front of the wing built at a ninety-degree angle to the main wing, which contains the entrance. At the front, granite steps lead up to a deeply shaded wraparound porch. The entrance itself is guarded by tall wrought iron gates. Where the two wings meet at the back of the house, some wild wag added a gothic conservatory with glass walls and a peaked glass roof, accessible from the narrow picture gallery and the black walnut paneled library.

The oldest house in the development, it is perhaps a tad self-conscious of its dated pretention, but in its defense, it lacks the self-satisfaction of the rather pedestrian split levels—themselves ignorant of the fact they were simply the unfortunate spawn of *The Brady Bunch*—that are its neighbors.

The house, for all its majesty, is deceptive, though: the roof that slopes over the house, the wing, and the two towers all conspire to hide the fact that it is only one room deep.

"What do you think?" the realtor asked.

Jackson gazed at the black-walnut-coffered ceiling soaring eleven feet above our heads and, glancing at my enraptured expression, said, "I think we'd like to make an offer."

Friday, April 25, 2014, Janus—We moved into our new house this afternoon. By dinner, we had been visited by Kitt, a warrior princess in braids, with bangled earrings, a nose ring, and a chip on her shoulder. She was dressed completely in black: black clingy pants with flared legs and a charcoal T-shirt with "We were NOT all Kung Fu fighting" emblazoned in a lighter gray across her chest. Kitt introduced herself as the sole board member of the Homeowner Association. "So, I'm essentially a dictator," she explained blithely. "You can call me Queen K."

I was charmed. Jackson, irritated, clearly was not. She strutted about our new living room as if she owned it. Wheeling around, she said, "I take it you're a couple?"

I nodded; Jackson ignored her.

"Good. It's nice to have *family* in the neighborhood."

Her peculiar emphasis on the word "family" was odd until I caught her drift. Our warrior princess is a lesbian. Also, we learned, without asking, vegan, in recovery, and mad at the world.

"Y'all are cute," she pronounced looking at us as if we were curiosities in a notions shop, or maybe a special exhibit at the local zoo. "How long have you been together?"

When I told her, she raised an eyebrow.

"We've been together since high school. *Literally*," Jackson said, clearly, inexplicably, annoyed.

"Well, I'll let you get back to unpacking," she said, still watching us curiously.

"By the way," she said as she waltzed to our front door, again as if it was her front door. "Your grass is an inch and a half longer than regulation."

Jackson and I looked at each other. "She measured?" he mouthed to me.

"I know you just moved in, so I'll give you until tomorrow to come into compliance. Otherwise, I'll have to fine you."

"But we just moved in."

"I know, that's why I'm giving you until tomorrow—"

"But we don't have a lawn mower yet."

"A pair of scissors will do the job." She slammed the front door and was gone.

I looked at Jackson, who was walking towards the kitchen.

"I need a drink," he called over his shoulder. "Do you want one?"

"Yes, please," I answered, trailing him, feeling like the survivor of a tornado or a hurricane who hasn't yet surveyed the damage wrought and so has no idea what that particular visitation has cost them.

"What do you think of Kitt?" I asked Jackson as we brushed our teeth—our new master bathroom has double sinks, so we'll no longer have to jockey for position to rinse and spit.

He rinsed and spit into his sink. "Let's see, she's lesbian, vegan, alcohol-free, angry—we'll get along great!"

"Oh, she's not that bad," I said, moving to the toilet to pee.

"I sense danger," he said.

"What?" I asked. As the sound of my peeing echoed off the honed marble floor and walls, I thought about how far we'd come.

"I said, 'We in danger, girl!'"

"Oh, stop!" I laughed.

"Let's go to bed," he said, kissing my cheek.

"Give me a few minutes," I said, shaking off. "I want to write in my journal."

He shrugged.

"Wait up for me, though," I said.

He looked at me and laughed. "Oh, someone wants to get laid."

"Well, it *is* our first night in our new house. We need to celebrate."

"Fine," he said. "If I'm asleep, wake me."

Wednesday, April 30, 2014, Janus—Kitt stopped by today to thank us for cutting the grass and to drop off a binder full of HOA rules and regulations. She sat on the couch and made small talk, which I always find exhausting. Finally, she said, "Well, I should be going..." while making no effort to get up and go.

"Yes," Jackson said, standing, surprising me. He is rarely direct or confrontational.

"What do y'all do?" Kitt asked, ignoring him.

"Pretty much as we please, being adults and all," Jackson said.

I glanced at Jackson and said, "I'm always confused when people ask that question, as if knowing what I do to pay the mortgage tells you anything about me."

Now it was Kitt's turn to be annoyed. "If you think by being coy about your job you're being discreet, you're wrong."

"We're not being discreet," Jackson said in a peeved tone. "We're politely telling you what we do isn't any of your business."

Barely glancing at him, Kitt continued as if Jackson hadn't spoken. "This house, that *watch* Jackson is wearing—a vintage Vacheron Constantin, the art deco model with special logs, I believe—tells me everything you're attempting to obscure."

When we glanced at her in surprise, Jackson staring at his watch, she said, "I'm a jewelry appraiser at an auction house. See? Not a hard question to answer. Well, I really *must* be going," she said as if we'd been keeping her. She rose to her feet and swiftly left.

Sunday, May 11, 2014, Janus—Jackson and I were out front, attempting to plant in the rocky, inhospitable soil under the living room window, when Jackson glanced up and muttered with dismay, "Here comes the angry Amazon."

"What?" Then I saw Kitt striding towards us, dressed all in black, her shadowed face like a storm cloud.

"You know," she said before we could acknowledge her, "I didn't think anyone would ever buy this…folly."

Rubbing sweat from our eyes, we looked up at her.

"It's such an eyesore," she continued tactlessly. "For years, we tried to have it torn down, but it was during all that historic preservation hysteria, so no go."

"I'm glad," I said.

Shielding his eyes against the sun, Jackson remarked, "You know where we come from, folks considered us an eyesore. They would have torn *us* down if they could have."

Kitt, seemingly stung by Jackson's words, looked at us appraisingly. "Indeed," she said before starting back across the lawn. She stopped abruptly and wheeled around.

"Seriously, though, why *this* house?" she asked.

"It's the perfect house for us," Jackson said. "You see Oren identifies as an impoverished English Lord keeping up appearances."

While I tried to choke back laughter, Kitt wrinkled her brow. Whether in confusion or disapproval at Jackson's clear mocking of identity politics, I couldn't tell. Looking at him, she asked, "And you? You're Alec Scudder to his Maurice?"

I bristled at her implying that Jackson was somehow less than I.

"Oh, yes. I'm definitely Scudder to his Maurice."

I looked at him in surprise. I'd found a tattered paperback of the E.M. Forster novel in the campus used bookstore sophomore year, after I'd discovered and read Patricia Nell Warren's *The Front Runner* and *The Fancy Dancer*. Since then, I'd read the novel repeatedly, obsessively. Our second Christmas together,

Jackson had given me a pristine leather-bound edition, which had started my collection of books, but as far as I knew, he'd only seen the movie once.

"Climbing in his window nightly to reclaim him?" Kitt continued archly.

"No. No need for windows or doors," Jackson said, "when you dwell in each other's heart."

Realizing Jackson was her match, Kitt turned and stormed away. Taking her place, a ragged black cat with an angry-looking scar on his forehead hissed at us. "Frankenstein, come," Kitt barked without turning around. The cat cast us a baleful glance then stalked away behind Kitt on its silent cat feet.

Rising, I said, "I need a drink. How about you?"

"Just water," Jackson answered, looking lost as if he'd been cast adrift in Kitt and Frankenstein's wake.

"She didn't come back, did she?" I asked, returning, glancing around cautiously.

"No," Jackson said as he hacked furiously at an obstinate root. I handed him a tumbler of water.

"She's something," I said. "And that cat."

Jackson nodded, leaning back on his heels and drinking greedily from the sweating glass.

"It's so hot. I don't understand how she can walk around wearing all that black."

"The devil doesn't feel the heat," Jackson said, laying his glass on the grass and once again taking up siege against the obstinate root.

Saturday, June14, 2014, Janus—I watched Jackson, standing in front of the mirror, gather his braids in one hand and sweep them upward deftly before slipping a rubber band around them to form a ponytail high up on his head. He caught me looking at him in the mirror. "You get more beautiful every year," I said walking up behind him and kissing his neck.

He laughed; our eyes met in the mirror. "And your eyesight gets worse every year."

Jackson seems to have amassed a fan club. He makes a habit of assisting everyone in the neighborhood—mostly the single older women, but he helps the men, too, fixing shutters and cutting down trees. And of course, being a master plumber, he is a wiz at unclogging toilets and changing faucets and hot water heaters.

The men seem to like him, but the women adore him. "You're so lucky," they coo, while sighing over Jackson. *He's so helpful. Jackson is so handsome.* I'd hear these adjectives, this gushing adoration, and wonder who they were talking about. For when I think of Jackson, I think simply, *he's mine.* And in that thought is all the love and pride and gratitude I have for Jackson. And surety that we are meant to be, that we will be together always.

Friday, July 4, 2014, Janus—Kitt seems to appreciate men. "He's a cutie," she'll say about the UPS guy, or comment, "He's hot," about our weightlifter neighbor. Once she said about some actor or other, "He's so fine, I would drink his bath water." Now there's an image I'll never get out of my head! Usually, I agree with her; we seem to share a type, as much as a lesbian can have a type of man, anyway.

I am always surprised by her comments on men. I mean, what kind of lesbian notices *men*? Her view of men is oddly chauvinistic, as if a man's only value is an aesthetic one. She never comments on their personalities or sense of humor. In her mind, men fall into two categories: comely objects and unbeautiful ones who require no comment or recognition. This isn't true of Jackson, though. She sighs and fawns over him, singing his praises to me. "He's so good, you're so lucky," she often says. If Jackson has his fans, Kitt is the president of his fan club. When I tell Jackson Kitt was fangirling over him again, he just grunts.

Tonight, the three of us were in the conservatory waiting for the fireworks to start. With its glass walls and ceiling, the conservatory is a perfect spot to catch the fireworks display, even if the windows do rattle a bit in their steel frames from the noise. Jackson and I were sharing a bottle of wine; Kitt was swigging flavored seltzer water as if it was gin. Jackson laid his head against my shoulder then snuck a kiss on my neck.

"I can't believe you two have been together forty-odd years," Kitt said. "Aren't you bored of each other by now?"

I was too startled by the sharpness of the question, by its bitter edge, to respond. Jackson lifted his head from my shoulder and grinned at her. "Have you *met* Oren? Every day, he surprises me—with a thought, or a book he's read, or the million and one ways he shows me he loves me. I'd never felt loved before I met him. Even now, forty-odd years later as you say, I'm sure he's the only person who's ever loved me."

"That's not true," Kitt murmured, looking away from us.

The first fireworks lit up the sky, distracting us from Kitt's sudden unhappiness.

Saturday, August 2, 2014, Janus—In college, my work-study job was with the Office of Residential Living. In addition to answering the phones and filing, I was charged with planning events that "foster a sense of community," which simply meant commandeering the rooftop lounge and stocking the room with food and non-alcoholic drink.

On his days off, Jackson would often stop by to "volunteer." I suspected he simply wanted to be with me, in this, my other world that didn't revolve around him. No one minded his presence. Everyone was charmed by our coupledom, that we were so out and open and clearly adored each other. One Friday, we were assigned to go pick up a party tray and cookies from the caterer—A Moveable Feast. I swear the university was their only customer. On our way out the building, Jackson commandeered a wheelchair, sat down and insisted I push him to the caterer.

A Moveable Feast is located in a narrow, crumbling rowhouse several steep steps up from the sidewalk. I locked the brakes on the wheelchair and left Jackson sitting in the sun.

Noticing him, the owner, a kind, pale, motherly type, said, "We have a wheelchair ramp in the back. You can bring your friend in."

Glancing out the window at Jackson, sitting in the sun, inspecting his nails, I said, "Nah. I've pushed that cripple all over campus. I'm tired. He can stay out there in the sun. He needs the vitamin D."

The kindly mother grew paler still, her fingers fumbling against the aluminum foil.

On the way back to campus, the tray of sandwiches and warm cookies in his lap, I related the story to Jackson, who whooped and hollered as if he'd won the lottery.

This all came rushing back to me today in Target, when I turned around from looking at birthday cards to find Jackson had climbed into our cart.

"Get out," I laughed.

"No," he said. "Push me."

"Jackson," I warned.

"Push me," he insisted. "Please."

"Fine," I said, giving up and pushing the cart, now impossibly heavy with him in it. At the self-checkout, everyone discreetly stared at us, at a grown man sitting in a cart and another grown man calming pushing him. A couple of kids pointed and giggled; their embarrassed parents slapped their hands down. Jackson was, of course, delighted. When I reached between his legs for the last item in the cart, besides him, he leaned over and kissed me. Watching us, the entire line of people erupted into cheers. *God, I thought, I love this man.*

It was only as we were loading the car that it dawned on me how far we'd come.

Monday, September 1, 2014, Janus—Jackson and I were working in near-silent tandem, setting up for the Homeowner Association's annual Labor Day cookout. He was lighting the grill—hardwood coal, not gas; "Real men use charcoal, not gas," Jackson insisted in his best gay voice to all who would listen—as I poured sangria and chunks of ice and watermelon into an enormous cut-glass art deco punchbowl. Some sangria splashed against the immaculate cuts on the bowl's exterior; I grabbed a damp paper towel and polished it to its highly reflective luster.

"You love that punchbowl, don't you?" Jackson said building his charcoal tower. I hadn't realized he was watching me.

I'd admired it in the window of an antique store for months, wanting to buy it but unable to justify its cost. I'd talked to Jackson about it incessantly. Finally, he'd surprised me by buying it for me.

"I can't believe you bought me this," I'd exclaimed, unwrapping the unexpected midweek gift.

"Why not?" he'd asked. "You deserve it. You deserve beauty. You deserve *everything*."

"I do," I admitted now. "Thank you for giving it to me."

"No need to thank me," Jackson said. "Not when you've given *me* everything."

"Do you two ever fight?" Kitt asked suddenly.

Her question startled me. I'd forgotten she was there. None of the homeowners wanted to deal with her any more than was absolutely necessary, so Kitt "voluntold" us to help because she couldn't do it alone.

"Yeah, of course," I said. "But rarely."

"And when we do we make up."

"How?" Kitt seemed genuinely curious.

"I start walking his way and he starts walking mine," Jackson said.

"Ain't no road too long when you meet in the middle," I finished.

Jackson squeezed my shoulder and, standing on his tippy toes, kissed the top of my head.

"Ah, more country wisdom," Kitt said derisively before adding more aggressively, "Why do you two continue to play at being simple country boys when you're clearly not. You lead a good life, you have this *charmed romance*..."

"We don't pretend to be country boys," I said. "We *are* country boys. Like coal under pressure becomes a diamond, we became who we are—who you see—under the pressure of growing up when we did, where we did, surrounded by the ignorant people who lived there with us." And I believed what I said was true, even as I understood every accolade, every promotion, every raise I earned, every watch I bought Jackson pushed us farther from where we'd grown up, who we were told we needed to be.

"I can't with you two," Kitt said.

The first of the neighbors began to arrive; Kitt retreated to her house.

The afternoon skipped along easily enough. There was more than enough food and plenty of neighborly banter. Kitt was nowhere to be seen, leaving Jackson and I to act as hosts. Our delicately wrought tranquility was nearly shattered, though, when one six-year-old, seeing Kitt emerge from her garage, fairly shouted, "Uh-oh. Here comes Kittzilla," which statement was met with a furious chorus of, "Shhh!"

Kittzilla—that's what the reluctant members of the HOA call Kitt behind her back, which is to say always because they seldom speak to her face-to-face.

Kitt sauntered over smiling, and everyone smiled, relieved, in return. As it turned out, we'd avoided one catastrophe only to career straight into another.

I was talking to Simon, our newest neighbor, who had just moved into the house at the apex of the cul-de-sac yesterday evening. Kitt walked over to where we stood at the punchbowl and proceeded to introduce herself to Simon.

Looking up at her, he inexplicably blurted, "Shit, you're tall."

Kitt looked down at him and said, "Since we seem to be stating the obvious, may I say, shit, you're an ill-mannered, fat, little troll."

His mouth fell open as if the springs that had held his smile in place had suddenly broken. Stifling a laugh, I quickly poured him a cup of sangria. He took it, his mouth still hanging open, and waddled towards Jackson and the grill.

As we were getting ready for bed last night, Jackson said, "We survived the cookout."

"Indeed, we did—no thanks to that kid. Or Kitt." Then, remembering our earlier conversation with Kitt, I asked him, "Does it sometimes feel like Kitt resents us for...*being us?*"

"Sometimes?" Jackson asked, rolling his eyes and kissing me goodnight. He lay down and rolled onto his side, facing away from me, and immediately reached behind to pull me against him. Tonight, he clearly wanted to be the "little spoon." I promptly forgot about Kitt and snuggled against him.

ROSE GOLD (2015)

Sunday, April 12, 2015, Janus—Kitt has a type—fairly butch, muscular, indifferent—which seems entirely wrong for her and always, predictably, ends in heartbreak. When she is dating, Kitt becomes withdrawn, mild-mannered, almost meek, allowing the other woman to make all decisions and boss her around.

This morning, she came over before breakfast after her latest breakup, which apparently occurred around dawn. Just after midnight, we'd heard yelling from her house across the street, followed by the slamming of doors. Just before sunrise, we'd been awakened by the gunning of an engine; there came the crunch of gravel, the screech of tires hitting asphalt at high speed, then... silence.

"And another one bites the dust," Jackson had murmured, pulling me against him. So, neither of us was surprised when Kitt knocked on our door just after Jackson put coffee on.

Kitt was inconsolable, crying literally on my shoulder. "Why? *Why* does no one love me?" she wailed.

Why indeed, I wondered. Kitt is an attractive woman, others— mostly women—tell me constantly, though MJ once described her as looking like a cross between a corpse and a kewpie doll. Which I understood; Kitt's self-blended foundation makes it appear she has powdered her face with chocolate wine, her emphatic black eyebrows are drawn on, and her tiny, enflamed mouth is reminiscent of the iconic doll. Makeup aside, Kitt is tall, broad-shouldered, fit, and well-proportioned.

Jackson offered to make breakfast. "I can't eat," she screamed.

"Want some orange juice?" I asked, extricating myself from her embrace and standing. "I'm about to make mimosas. Or maybe I'll make Kir Royales."

"How can you two *drink* at this hour?" she asked, sniffling.

"You know what? I think I'm just gonna have Champagne," I said, even as I thought maybe I'd have a French 75 instead since Kitt's histrionics were rapidly pushing my mood beyond the soothing capabilities of Champagne alone. I wondered idly how I could get some gin into Kitt. After all, gin started its life as a tonic to ease anxiety—I like to think of it as a primitive precursor to Xanax.

Kitt left abruptly; either her grief had washed away with her tears, or she'd grown bored with us. I walked into the kitchen where Jackson was frying bacon and scrambling eggs. "Well, that was unexpected," I said.

"I know," Jackson agreed. "Who knew she had tear ducts?"

I smacked his arm and handed him a French 75. Giggling, I said, "She says she's done with women, says they suck."

"I doubt it," Jackson said, emptying eggs and bacon onto plates. "I mean, what are they allegedly sucking?"

I giggled again, the Champagne and gin having gone straight to my head. He placed a plate in front of me. "I adore you," I said.

"Of course, you do," he said, kissing the top of my head. "I feed you and I don't weep on your shoulder about women while simultaneously judging you for drinking before noon."

"Kitt has the worst taste in women."

"Worst taste? She has none at all," Jackson said, sitting down across from me.

I gulped my drink then poured myself another glass from the pitcher. "Still," I said, "at least this last one—what was her name?"

"Anastasia," Jackson said. "Or maybe it was Nancy."

"Well, at least," I insisted drunkenly, "Anastasia/Nancy was an improvement over Theodora."

Jackson grunted noncommittally as he began to eat.

Kitt had been dating Theodora when we moved into our house. She had met Theodora—who at the time went by the name "Ten," an homage to her own flawlessness, which was magnified by her cleanly shaven head and a sly nod to the movie of the same name that starred Bo Derrick in a bikini and, bizarrely, *cornrows*—at Girlfriends, the oldest lesbian bar in the country. Girlfriends was an anachronism, a throwback to WACs and the Andrew Sisters and perpetually on life support due to its aging decrepitude and its owners' refusal to change anything. As aged and decrepit as the bar itself, they refused to sign a Do Not Resuscitate order each time bankruptcy approached. Through the collective strength of their lesbian resolve, the bar would survive each financial crisis.

Theodora Ten was a lesbian anarchist. Kitt had adored her instantly. She'd moved into Kitt's house a few weeks after they met. Almost immediately, nightly, Ravel's *Boléro*—all fifteen-and-a-half minutes of it—could be heard drifting out of Kitt's bedroom window. It was only after six months or so that another dimension to Theodora had emerged. That is, she suffered from Dissociative Personality Disorder. She had two alters: Stella, a loose woman and sometimes sex worker in a blonde "mermaid" wig, and Beatrice, the church lady.

Theodora cheerfully refused all treatment, preferring to give her alters their freedom and right to life. Thus, she regularly, unpredictably cycled through her personalities, whom she referred to collectively as "the Tens," donning a blonde wig and applying bold red lipstick when Stella suddenly chose to appear and snatching it off her bald head when Theodora or Beatrice reasserted herself. The problem was occasionally, she'd go to bed Theodora but wake up Beatrice, naked beside Kitt, whereupon she would pull a heavy Bible out of her purse and begin beating Kitt with it while praying for her immortal soul. After one too many Bible-induced black eyes and yet another fractured rib, Kitt had called it quits.

The one time we'd had dinner with them, Jackson had leaned heavily against the door after they'd left, and panted, "*What* was that? I feel like I'm drunk."

"I feel," I said into the suddenly still evening, "like I'm just coming off a three-day bender."

When Kitt came over crying after her breakup with Theodora, or rather the Tens since presumably she'd dumped all three of them, Jackson said, "You deserve better, someone who is—I don't know—*not insane*, maybe?"

"Oh, it's easy for you to judge, isn't it?" she accused. "After all, what do either of you know about how hard it is to find someone… *compatible*? You each found 'the one' right out of grade school!"

"Actually, it was high school," Jackson said.

I glared at him, and Frankenstein, who seemed as committed to misery as Kitt, hissed at us.

Friday, June 26, 2015, Rehoboth Beach—Today, Jackson and I were in Rehoboth checking out our favorite shops on the main drag, eating ice cream cones and waiting for cocktail hour. Both our phones started pinging almost simultaneously. We ignored them—we were on vacation and feeling very removed from our day-to-day lives. MJ called. I recognized her ring tone, so I answered. Jackson pulled out his phone to scroll through his messages.

"Hey, MJ," I said, between licks of ice cream.

"We won," she shouted.

"Won what?"

She started to cry. "The Supreme Court ruled in favor of marriage equality."

"What?" I dropped my ice cream. I'd completely forgotten *today was the day.*

"Holy shit!" Jackson shouted. "The Supreme Court just made same sex marriage the law of the land."

"When are you two getting married?" MJ asked in my ear as I stared at Jackson, trying to decipher his reaction, and then saw tears coursing down his cheeks as he embraced me.

"Everyone is texting me asking when we're getting married."

Cars driving down the street blew their horns; people on the sidewalks whooped and hollered and hugged strangers. Jackson and I, caught in the maelstrom of excitement and disbelief, hugged each other.

"MJ, let me call you back. I need to check the news."

"Be sure you're near a TV. It's our lead story tonight." And she was gone.

A few minutes later, Claude texted me:

Let us know when you two are getting married. We would be honored to host your reception at our house. It will be our gift to you both. Just let us know the date. We'll take care of everything else.

Hugs & Kisses,
Claude & Octavio

Saturday, August 8, 2015, Janus—Jackson and I are getting married. It's all we've talked about since leaving Rehoboth. We've settled on August 28 as the date, so we've been shopping for wedding bands—Cartier, Tiffany, Van Cleef & Arpels. Today, we decided nothing appealed to us, so we are opting to exchange the same heavy platinum Atlas rings from Tiffany & Co. we gave each other nearly three decades ago on our tenth anniversary. Back then, we'd taken the precious rings out of their dark velvet boxes and placed them on each other's fingers at the jewelry counter. The saleswoman witnessing the exchange wished us *mazel tov*, and we'd gone to dinner at the hottest Cuban restaurant in the city. This time around, there would be an actual marriage license and a justice of the peace and MJ and her parents as witnesses—we had no family and no church, so a justice of the peace ceremony seemed a reasonable option—and a reception with friends, hosted by Claude and Octavio.

Saturday, August 29, 2015, Janus—Yesterday, Jackson and I got married. We'd originally planned to go to a justice of the peace with MJ as our witness, but she convinced us to marry at City

Hall in the chambers of a judge she and Octavio knew. She also wanted to film our wedding for a news story.

MJ arrived in a town car to pick us up at 4:15. She emerged from the car's shadowy depths wearing a circa 1970s Halston crystal and pearl beaded black silk chiffon jacket with a matching skirt. The heavily beaded jacket was open at the front and had long bishop sleeves, which were gathered at the wrist. She looked stunning: understated and elegant. MJ studied us each in turn from the bottom of the porch steps. Jackson was wearing a midnight-blue tuxedo with a silk shawl collar that flattered his litheness while making his shoulders look broader. I was wearing a lavender linen suit with a mint-green silk bow tie with lavender flowers that Jackson had bought for me one morning in Italy when he'd gone out to get us coffee.

"You're both gorgeous," MJ pronounced. Then, turning around and offering us each an arm, she said, "Shall we go, gentlemen?"

As I slid into the seat next to her, Jackson leaned in and asked, "Where are Claude and Octavio?"

"They're meeting us there."

Getting in, Jackson asked MJ, "You're alone?"

"No. I'm with the two of you."

"No," Jackson said in the teasing tone he tends to adopt with MJ, "I thought you might have had a plus-one."

"Why would I need a plus-one when I have the two of you?" she asked, straightening her already perfect posture. MJ has always been notoriously tight-lipped about her love life. In college, she'd been in a few *entanglements*—boys like glancing blows to her heart. She in her turn, I was sure, had bruised, if not altogether broken, a few others.

We fell silent as we walked through City Hall's whispering grandeur, feeling the weight of what was about to happen. We were getting married; what had always seemed an impossibility suddenly wasn't.

"Mary Jane," a voice boomed pleasantly, causing her name to ricochet around the marble columns supporting a terra cotta ceiling.

"Mister Mayor," MJ responded, turning around. The mayor kissed her cheek. "Let me introduce you to my friends, Oren and Jackson. Jackson, Oren, His Honor the Mayor."

"A pleasure, a pleasure," he said to each of us in turn in his booming voice while taking our hands in his and looking us in the eye before covering our hand with his free hand. Noticing the cameraman trailing us at a carefully calculated distance so that he was present but not intrusive, he asked, "Where are you off to, Mary Jane?"

"We're headed to Judge McAfee's chambers—he's going to marry these two."

"Wonderful. Mazel tov," he said, looking at us then, turning to MJ, added, "I know the judge—wonderful man. I've an idea. What if instead of the judge, I perform the ceremony?" He looked at us. We looked at MJ.

"I'll leave that decision to you two," MJ said.

The mayor has always supported LGBTQ folks and marches in the parade every year; he was an early supporter of marriage equality. It is rumored that his daughter is a lesbian. She'd come out to her parents young and then swore them to secrecy. I think on some level he hoped marrying us in a public way would encourage her to open up. Also, he never met a camera he didn't like.

"OK," we said. "If you're sure Judge McAfee won't be offended."

As we waited for the mayor to get ready, Jackson, silent and still, held my hand tightly as he was afraid I'd fly away. I looked around the room. It was warm; its polished oak-paneled walls gleamed. High above our heads was an elaborate plaster ceiling, stenciled in gold leaf and enamel; cherubs, sexless, ageless, holding garlands of laurel, cuddled in each of the ceiling's four corners. I was reminded of our first date—that picnic in the countryside—when I'd imagined Cupid sitting in the trees shooting love's arrows at us. I felt tears pricking the corners of my eyes. MJ, who knows me well, touched my arm. "It's hard to believe we're here, isn't it?"

I nodded, afraid to speak, not trusting my voice not to tremble, not wanting to cry through my vows.

"Gentlemen, are we ready?" the mayor asked, emerging into the room through a door notched into the paneling I hadn't noticed before.

Standing in front of the mayor listening to his words, none of which I can now remember, I felt...not nervous—after all, I've been with Jackson my entire adult life—but giddy with excitement. We repeated the vows the mayor spoke. We—or rather I—had opted not to write our own vows. Having been together as long as we had, we'd surely said everything we had to, to each other. Standard vows had been sufficient for generations before us, and they'd be sufficient for us. Besides, I told myself, this was just a legal formality and had little to do with our love for each other.

Then it was time to exchange rings, and my thoughts changed. Jackson slipped my ring on my finger, promising to love and cherish me forever. Jackson's ring has spent most of its life on a thin platinum chain around his neck; his being a union plumber wearing a wedding ring without a visible wife had seemed both unwise and potentially dangerous at the time. Today, I proudly slipped his ring on his finger, knowing it would stay there this time.

Winding down, the mayor said, "I now pronounce you husbands."

Turning to each other, holding each other's hands, we said simultaneously, "And we shan't be parted no more, and that's finished."

"You may kiss," the mayor said. I opened my eyes to soft flashes, cheers, and the feel of Jackson's lips on mine. Claude was crying, as was MJ. Octavio smiled and slapped us on the back. He and Claude left to make sure everything was ready for us at the house.

Because we didn't need to be at our reception until seven, MJ arranged for us to stop at Indigo for a glass of Champagne. I thought nothing of it when the host had us wait in the vestibule while he conferred with MJ before leading her away.

He came back to get us. On the threshold into the bar, he paused and said, "Ladies and gentlemen, please join us in welcoming new husbands, Oren and Jackson." There was applause. In the murky lavender light, there were flashes of light, sparks in the dark from watches and bracelets and rings and the occasional set of flawlessly veneered teeth. MJ was already seated at our table. As we sat down, a pinpoint spotlight bathed our table in blue light. A waiter poured us each a glass of Belaire Bleu, their "house" Champagne—a blue-tinted French import said to have been inspired by the Riviera. "Please join us in a toast to the newlyweds," the host said, raising a glass. It was only then we noticed everyone in the bar was holding a glass of Champagne.

Turning to MJ, I said, "MJ—"

"Oh, hush," she said. "Drink up. We don't have a lot of time, and I refuse to leave a half-empty bottle behind."

Jackson squeezed my knee and touched his glass to mine. "You heard the lady. Drink up."

At her parents' house, MJ left us at the garden gate, instructing us to wait to enter until we heard the DJ announce us. Then we would walk in and dance the first dance together. At the end of the walkway leading to the backyard was an ice sculpture of two grooms holding each other. I was touched beyond words. The DJ said, "Everyone, please join us in welcoming the newlyweds, Oren and Jackson Strange." There was thunderous applause and then the opening music to King Floyd's "Groove Me" began to play. Claude had decided our reception should be a dance party and had installed a dance floor over the pool, so we knew dancing would be important. We'd decided our first dance would be sexy and sultry. Still, when Jackson took my hand, I was nervous.

As the song wound down, there were cheers and a few catcalls. Then things heated up when "Time of My Life" from *Dirty Dancing* began to play. We'd taken ballroom dancing classes for years when we lived in the city, and once we chose the songs for our first two dances, we'd returned to classes and practiced for weeks, memorizing the song's iconic dance moves. When Jackson spun away from me and went into his solo performance, I'd never in my life felt so proud, or so possessive. When his solo ended and he stood a few feet away from me, I launched myself into the air; he caught and held me aloft for moments before lowering me to the ground. It was possibly the most magical moment of my life. The DJ invited everyone to join us on the dance floor as he cued up "Feel This Moment" by Pitbull and Christina Aguilera.

The music faded and the dancing crowd dispersed, settling into their seats as MJ's TV voice filled the air. "Good evening, everyone. If I could just have you attention for a few minutes, I'd like to say a few words."

Sitting beside Jackson, trying to catch my breath, I looked around. The evening's décor was spare but elegant, all moody blues and winking white lights. Tables were covered in heavy black linen and white plates, whose silver rims caught and held the dancing white lights. Waitstaff, in crisp white shirts, formal pants, and satin cummerbunds, offered bellinis and canapés of every description.

There was silence, except for the rustling of fabric as people sat and turned their attention to MJ, and whispered thank-yous to the waitstaff handing out glasses of Champagne and collecting empty plates.

"Years ago," MJ began, "I was looking through Oren's parents' wedding album, and I asked him if he thought he'd ever get married. He said, 'What?'—if you know Oren, you know he starts every answer to a question with 'What?' as if he misheard you." This was followed by polite laughter and murmured agreement. "Then," MJ continued, "he said, 'No. Don't be ridiculous.' Oren is one of the smartest people I know, and he's often right in his opinions and predictions. I'm always pleased when he turns out to be right—I find his rightness reassuring. But in this instance, I am thrilled he was wrong." She raised the glass she held in her right hand and, raising her left hand in a Vulcan salute, palm forward, thumb extended, her fingers parted between her middle and ring finger, said, "To Oren and Jackson, may you live long and prosper."

Taking the microphone from MJ, Claude cleared her throat. "First, thank you *all* for joining us. When Octavio and I offered to host this reception, I knew from the start I wanted it to be more than a traditional reception. I wanted to it to be a true celebration of two extraordinary men, a testament to a great love it was our privilege to witness in its infancy, and a recognition of everything they've been through and overcome. That we have seen marriage equality become the law of the land and also to witness their marriage seems miraculous. Now, I'd like to make a toast to the newlyweds," she continued. On cue, waitstaff appeared with fresh trays of Champagne.

Claude paused as Octavio handed her a glass. "Here's to Jackson and Oren, who deserve all the happiness in the world."

Kitt said, perhaps more loudly than she'd intended and to no one in particular, "Why do they get a happy ending?"

"*What* did you just ask?" MJ demanded, turning towards her in a shiver of light and fury.

Kitt stepped back as if to place herself outside MJ's striking distance. Claude's maternal instincts must have picked up Kitt's vibrations because I saw her step from the podium and make her way towards us.

"I—I just was remarking on how lucky Jackson and Oren are to have found each other and gotten their happy ending…is all…"

"We've worked hard for this," Jackson said, taking my hand. "It's not like anyone wrote a fairy tale in the stars for us the day we were born."

Realizing her mistake and clearly not wanting to alienate Jackson, whom she adored, Kitt said, "I just meant you two are lucky—"

"Lucky?" Jackson practically shouted; Jackson, who never raises his voice. "Growing up when we did? Where we did? Until we met MJ and her family, O and I were all we had—"

"You have me, too," Kitt said looking at her feet.

"Everything OK?" Claude asked, walking up to us and seeing our tense faces and MJ's aggressive posture.

"Yes. Yes," MJ said. "Kitt was just telling us she has to leave, and we were just trying to convince her to stay a little longer."

"Oh, you must stay," Claude said. "We're about to serve dinner—"

"No, no," Kitt said. "So gracious of you, but I really must dash—"

"Bye, girl," MJ said, offering a saccharine smile before leaning forward and bussing the air on each side of Kitt's face.

"Yes, let me just grab my purse."

Nonplussed, Kitt turned in little circles, then followed Claude like a scolded puppy when Claude said, "Come, let me help you find your purse."

As MJ moved through the night, her skirt suit glowed like 10,000 fireflies. She had strung rhinestones through Jackson's braids, and as he moved his head sparks seemed to fly from his hair. In my pale-lavender suit, I glowed like phosphorus. Tonight, the three of us seemed not to just shimmer with light but to be light itself.

Dinner was over and the reception was winding down when Jackson stood as the DJ handed him the microphone. "Oren and I would like to thank Claude and Octavio and especially MJ for this evening. Our marriage license, our City Hall wedding has given us legal protection, recognition, safety, but this reception has given us family. For that, we thank you from the bottom of our hearts."

As Jackson spoke, unexpectedly, I noticed the waitstaff were again passing out glasses of Champagne. When the applause died down, Jackson raised his glass and said, "I'd like to make a toast to my husband—gosh, I never thought I'd ever be able to use the word 'husband' to describe the man I love—a man who, forty years ago had the opportunity to leave our shitty little provincial town. He could have gone alone. Instead, he chose to take me with him. O, thank you for giving me the time of my life."

Fighting tears and almost choking on love for Jackson, I whispered to MJ, who went to talk to the DJ. I stood, raising my glass. "To Jackson. Thank you for being my wings and my anchor." We touched glasses. "May I have this dance?" I asked. He looked perplexed because we hadn't rehearsed this. Still, he took my hand, and we made our way to the dance floor. He paused and threw his head back in laughter as he recognized the song the DJ had cued up: Aretha Franklin's "Son of a Preacher Man." I will carry that picture of Jackson in his midnight-blue tux, his head thrown back in laughter, with me always.

MJ was spending the night at her parents' house, so Jackson and I were to ride home alone. As we walked to the driveway with everyone following behind us, we discovered that the town car had been replaced by a lemon-yellow 1958 Buick Series 60 Century Convertible—the exact model my parents had ridden away from their own wedding in. It is the last photo in their wedding album. MJ has always loved that photo. On the trunk was written "Just Married," and tin cans had been tied to the rear bumper with ribbon in the colors of the rainbow.

"Oh, MJ!" I cried. "Where—"

"Later," MJ said, kissing me on the cheek. "Now go home with your husband."

From the backseat, as we looked over our shoulders at our friends lining the driveway, I noticed MJ's cameraman running behind the car with his camera.

At home, horny, half-drunk, and eager to consummate our new legal status, we started tossing off our clothes in the foyer that had at one time served as the house's portrait gallery. Portraits of the original owners' patriarchs and matriarchs stared down in stern disapproval at our discarded clothing.

We tumbled into bed. Naked. We assumed our respective positions and…fell asleep.

Sunday, September 6, 2015, Janus—On Monday's evening news, MJ congratulated us on our marriage and showed a highlight reel of our wedding and reception. This served as a teaser to the larger story that would be shown on the network's hour-long Sunday news wrap-up program.

The story that aired tonight profiled us and a lesbian couple who had been married by their fathers—a rabbi and a Presbyterian minister. The story focused on growing up and highlighted the differences between my and Jackson's experiences and those of the lesbian couple, who were in their late thirties, and how we'd felt before and after getting married, and the importance of straight allies.

The mayor, who of course was interviewed, said, *"Today, it was my great honor and privilege to marry two men, whom I'd only met minutes before their marriage. My understanding is that they hale from a rural part of our great state, where growing up, they didn't find the love or acceptance every child deserves. As a father, hearing that hurt me deeply. I hope that by joining them in holy matrimony today, I took a step toward correcting that wrong decades after the fact. And I want to send a clear message that I—and my administration—stand firm in the belief that every citizen deserves the same rights as every other citizen."*

The segment closed with a still photo of Jackson and me being driven away in the backseat of the Buick while looking back at the camera, the words *Just Married*, vivid against the car's bright-yellow paint, the cans tied to the rear bumper kicking up tiny sparks in the dark. MJ had brilliantly recreated the photo in my parents' wedding album. I thought of my parents and for the first time wondered if they would have been proud of the man I've become, if they would have loved Jackson.

After the program ended, wrestling with emotions even I couldn't articulate, I suggested we watch a movie. We settled on some confusing movie starring Sylvester Stallone and too much blood. More than an hour later, our landline rang as we were trapped in a movie-induced stupor. Our caller ID had announced it was Jackson's parents calling, so he put the call on speaker as he always does when they call so I can hear and he doesn't have to repeat the ugliness they spout. "At first," Reverend Jackson thundered, "I did not mind that boy—"

"Man. He hasn't been a boy in decades. He's a man—"

"That he led you astray. I was sure he'd lose his hold on you, and you'd return home and to the path of righteousness. And you could take over my ministry and truly show proof of God's grace—"

"The fact that Oren and I have been together for thirty-nine years despite people like you trying to tear us apart is proof of God's grace."

Through my sleepy haze, I heard shouting and what sounded like chanting. Even in my sleepy state, I clearly heard Reverend Jackson scream, "Your blasphemy I can overlook, but this is going too far."

"What are you talking about?" Jackson asked wearily.

"How dare you go on television and flaunt your wedding—" he spat the word "—embarrassing me."

"Embarrassing you? No one gives a shit about you. Least of all me."

"This is a travesty, not a marriage. It is a sterile union. There will never be children, therefore it is not a marriage in God's eyes!"

"*You* and *your* God can kiss my ass," Jackson shouted—Jackson who seldom curses and who *never* raises his voice. He laid the phone in its cradle gently as if afraid his anger by extension might otherwise damage it.

I attempted to sit up, knuckling sleep from my eyes. "What was that about?"

"I'm not sure. But I'm guessing they saw MJ's weekly wrap-up tonight."

"Oh. I assumed that was only aired locally."

"Apparently not. And they are an hour behind us, so it makes sense they must have just seen it."

"I can ask her. What was that noise in the background?"

"My mother praying and quoting scripture—Leviticus mostly."

"Oh," I said.

Sunday, September 13, 2015, Janus—Reverend Jack is dead. Jackson's mother called to tell him. The mighty warrior for Christ—her words—is dead, felled by an apparent heart attack in the middle of one of his fiery and thunderous sermons. The congregation had sat still for several minutes as he lay on the cold terrazzo floor, assuming he'd been overcome by passion and was gathering his strength before mounting the next sally against sin and fleshly corruption. A deaconess fanning him to cool his passion noticed his large, usually florid face and neck were turning blue and sounded the alarm.

"Are you going to the funeral?" I asked.

"Yes," Jackson said. "I need to see his lips sealed, his body removed from this earth."

I nodded. I too wanted to see him consigned to the darkness he'd wanted to condemn us to. But I knew Jackson's mother would object, and the gossip about Jackson and me would play like a bassline at the funeral. I didn't want to put Jackson in an awkward position, so I said, "I can't bring myself to go back there."

"I know," Jackson said. "You know, he never once hugged me? He said that's what made boys grow up to be sissies."

After we'd moved to the farm, I hadn't been touched without violence until I met Jackson. That's the kind of place we grew up in. Jackson and I hugged. Reverend Jack was dead. Though he had always been far away, it felt as if the air we were breathing had been cleared of a noxious gas.

Saturday, September 19, 2015, Janus—Jackson came back from Locust Hollow today, his father buried and his mother firmly in the care of the church deaconesses. He's only been gone a week, but I see a change in him. When he walked in the door, he seemed thinner, drawn, almost gaunt. And sad, which I would expect if anyone in his life other than Reverend Jack had died. He hugged me like he'd never let go. I eased him onto the sofa, making sure to sustain our physical contact.

"How did it go? How's your mother?"

"She said I shouldn't have come, that I was too late, that he, like Christ, had given his life to atone for my sin."

"She was talking about our marriage?"

He nodded. "I told her marrying you was the most natural thing in the world—the thing I wanted most—and that I wouldn't, *couldn't* change, even if I wanted to, which obviously, I don't."

"You never tried, though, did you?" Kitt asked.

Jackson started and so did I; he hadn't noticed her, and once I saw Jackson's state, I'd forgotten she was there.

"Tried what?" Jackson asked.

"To change."

Jackson pulled away from me and reeled back against the sofa's cushions as if Kitt had slapped him. "What?"

"I just mean…you and Oren were just teenagers when you…got together. Surely, it must have occurred to you at some point that there were other paths available to you?"

"What?" I asked.

Jackson, more tired than I'd ever seen him, asked wearily, "Haven't you said enough, Kitt?"

"I—I—I just meant—"

"Kitt," I said. "Please just…*go*." I'd tried to forgive her outburst at our reception and accepted at face value her excuse that she was a little drunk and still reeling from her recent breakup, a tad envious of our relationship and marriage but that she'd meant no harm. Now, I just wanted her gone, away from us.

She looked at me pleadingly. Frankenstein watched us with his crooked eyes. I jerked my head at her. *Just go.*

She turned to leave. Frankenstein, mewling unhappily, followed her.

"Kitt," Jackson said, surprising us both and stopping her in her tracks. When she turned around, her face was a beacon of hope. "You should know," Jackson said, "all paths lead to Oren."

She looked…vanquished.

Sunday, September 20, 2015, Janus—I threw my overnight bag in the back seat and climbed into the passenger seat next to MJ. "Thanks for the ride," I said by way of greeting.

"Anytime," MJ said, putting the car in gear and backing down the driveway. "But, where's Jackson?"

"He's in the house, sleeping. He just got back from Locust Hollow last night. He was there all week."

"Locust Hollow? Why on earth was he there? I didn't think either of you would ever go back there."

"His father died."

"Reverend Jack?"

I nodded.

"How do you feel? she asked.

"I'll quote Moms Mabley when she was asked how she felt about her ex-husband dying. 'I was raised to only say good of the dead. He's dead; good.'"

MJ chuckled and punched me in the arm. Turning serious, she asked, "How's Jackson?"

"Upset. Out of sorts. Evidently, his mother told him he killed his father."

"Let me guess, they saw the wedding story."

I nodded. "We didn't realize it was a national broadcast."

"Oh, sweetie, I'm sorry."

I shrugged. "It's fine. I hate to leave Jackson like this, though. But the client is threatening to cancel the contract, so I've got to go do damage control. I asked Jackson if he wanted to come with me, but he said no. It's only a couple of days."

"Want me to check on him for you?"

"No. He wants to be alone, I think. And Kitt said she'd keep an eye on him."

"I bet she will, that viper."

"MJ…"

"OK, fine. You know I don't trust that Amazonian heifer as far as I can throw her—"

"That's our exit!"

Sunday, December 6, 2015, Janus—I should have known today was going to be one of the worst days of my life this morning. Jackson was moodier and more distant than when he first came back from his father's funeral. This morning didn't start with sex as it usually does. In fact, our sex life dropped off about three months ago. I've tried to chalk it up to a combination of grief over Reverend Jack's death and age. Maybe I should try harder to restart our sex life, but he's rebuffed me the few times I've tried to initiate. I don't like asking anyone for anything. Not even Jackson. Not for *that*. No matter how lonely and horny I am. I've tried not to let sex's sudden absence chaff me.

We postponed grocery shopping yesterday because Jackson didn't feel like it. He didn't feel like it today either, even after I said he could ride in the cart, so I said I'd do the shopping alone. Hoping he'd change his mind, I pottered around the house and dragged my feet all day, so it was already dark when I left.

Shopping, I soon realized, was no fun without Jackson and his antics, so I decided we'd order pizza for dinner and headed home. I walked into the kitchen and discovered him and Kitt talking tensely at the kitchen table, heads together. Frankenstein was sitting placidly at Jackson's feet; over the last few months, they seem to have reached détente. He hissed at me, though, when I leaned down and kissed the top of Jackson's head.

"We have to tell him," Kitt said insistently.

"Tell who what?" I asked, setting my bags on the counter. They both jumped a little at the question.

"What are you doing back so soon?" Jackson asked. "I thought you were going shopping."

"I was, but I changed my mind. I picked up a couple of bottles of wine. I figured we could order pizza. So, what's up?" I asked, pulling a bottle out and hunting for the corkscrew.

"I'm pregnant," Kitt said.

"Jackson, where's the corkscrew? You're pregnant? I never knew you wanted kids."

"I didn't. This was an accident."

"Oh. Have you told the father?" I noticed Jackson squirming in his seat and staring at the tabletop as if it held the secret to the meaning of life.

"Yes. He knows."

"Oh, OK. Who is he?"

"Jackson."

"Jackson?" I repeated, pulling the corkscrew out of a jumbled drawer in triumph.

"Jackson is," Kitt blurted.

I returned to the table with the open bottle of wine and two glasses. "No wine for you, Missy, not in your condition," I said teasingly, waggling a finger at her. "Jackson is what?" I asked sitting.

"The father. Of my baby. Jackson is the father of my baby."

"You donated sperm to her?" I asked looking at him. "Without telling me?"

"No," Kitt said, even though I hadn't addressed her.

"I don't understand," I said. "You're pregnant and Jackson is the father? How did that happen?"

"Oh, sweetie, I know sex ed was lacking back in Smallville, but surely, they managed to cover the basics of how babies are made—"

"Jesus Christ, Kitt!" Jackson snapped, then to me, "Oren—"

"You're sleeping with my husband?" I asked Kitt in disbelief. Then to Jackson, "You're sleeping with *her*?"

Jackson moved his hand suddenly as if out of reflex he was reaching out to steady me. I stared at the rose-gold Breitling on his wrist—his "everyday" watch—the one I'd given him for his fortieth birthday. I can't explain why, except I felt if I concentrated hard enough, I could not only stop its Swiss movement but force it back in time five minutes, to the time before life as I knew it ended, pushing us to the other side of this apocalypse. I've always disliked winter when everything warm and colorful has gone and there is nothing but frozen ground below and windswept sky barren of warmth above; it had never occurred to me that I would die on a winter evening and be left to rot on a pyre of ice.

Jackson caught himself, pulled his hand away, then excused himself to go to the bathroom. He looked like he was about to cry or vomit. I watched him leave then, turning to Kitt, said, "I don't understand how this happened."

"Of course you understand how this happened," Kitt said. "You're not that naïve."

"I thought you were supposed to be a lesbian."

She shrugged. "I sweat with women. I sweat with men."

"So, you're what you young people call fluid now?"

"I guess. You know I've always wanted what you had."

"I knew that, yes. But I didn't think you literally wanted what I had as in *my husband*."

She shrugged again. Jackson returned.

"I'm tired," I said, standing. Sighing wearily, overdramatically, I knew, I added, "We can sort this out tomorrow. I'm going to bed. You can see yourself out," I added, looking pointedly at Kitt. Turning to Jackson, I asked rhetorically, "You coming?" quite as if the impossible hadn't just happened and he'd never accompany me to bed again.

When neither of them said anything, I felt as if I'd stepped back a little, outside myself, looking at us in a mirror. The mirror cracked; out of the crack emerged Kitt with her swollen, pregnant belly, Jackson at her side.

"Blue Moon?" I said, unsure of him for the first time in my life. "Blue Moon?"

He winced at the old nickname. I hadn't called him that in ages.

"You go ahead," Jackson said finally. "I'm staying with Kitt."

I watched as she covered his hand with hers. Tears stung my eyes and the sour in my stomach made its way to my throat, burning all the way. I stumbled out of the kitchen, feeling the bruises start to rise and burn quite as if my brothers and grandfather had turned on me again, determined to beat my love for Jackson out of me.

Monday, December 7, 2015, Janus—When I staggered out of bed today, it was nearly noon. I never sleep that late—not even at the weekend. Today is a weekday. I called out sick at work. *Fuck them*, I thought, *they'll get over it.* I'm never late; I never call in sick. And as founder emeritus, I have unexercised privileges. Besides, it was late, and my head throbbed. I was no doubt dehydrated, and probably hungover. Unable to sleep, I'd opened a couple of bottles of aged claret and drunk directly from the bottles; I couldn't be bothered to pour the precious contents into the Riedel wineglasses I'd bought specifically for it. I'd been saving the wine—hoarding it really—for a special occasion. If the ending of life as I knew it isn't a special occasion, I don't know what is. I'd drunk greedily and now I was paying the price.

I needed coffee but had no idea how to make it. Coffee was Jackson's domain. He always made it using a complicated recipe involving fresh ground beans, chicory, and eggshells. I made my way to the kitchen, hoping to find instant coffee in a cabinet. I was stopped by the smell of brewing coffee. On the stove, hot fresh coffee bubbled. On the counter beside the stove was a box of chocolate croissants, neatly tied with red and white twine, and my favorite mug. Beneath the mug was a note in Jackson's neat hand. It was instructions for making coffee.

After drinking two cups of coffee, I went back to bed, unable to face this new reality in which Jackson was missing. When I awoke again, it was twilight and Jackson was in the room, gathering clothes from the closet and dressers. My fatigued brain thought for a moment he was back and putting away laundry, but no, he was stuffing clothes into contractor bags—why? For God's sake, we have *luggage*! I sat up.

"Use a suitcase," I said.

"Why? I'm only going across the street."

I slumped back down, exhausted. "Thanks for the coffee this morning," I said. When he didn't answer, I asked, "What happened?"

"I don't know," he said stubbornly.

"Another man—a *younger* man, I—I could understand," I said, "But *this...her*?"

He shrugged in that way he has that infuriates me, indicating as it does not indifference but confusion. If *he* didn't understand, how could I? And I *needed* to understand.

"Jackson…"

"I don't *know*." He sat on the bed, then sprang up as if he'd been burned. "I don't understand what happened any more than you do. All I know is from the time we were seventeen, I've loved you so completely there wasn't room for anything or anyone else. It's like you built a fortress around my heart—"

"What changed?"

"I don't know."

The walls of our love had started to crack, maybe from age, maybe from neglect, I thought. Then like rot, Kitt had crawled into those cracks and brought the whole structure down around my ears.

I sat up in bed. "I don't know how to let you—*us*—go," I said quietly, trying not to cry.

"You could stop the earth in its rotation if you wanted to, Oren. You can survive this. I know you can. I couldn't live with myself if I thought otherwise."

When I said nothing, he continued, "Listen, I have to go."

And just like that, he was gone, leaving me to wonder when exactly he had first left me.

Wednesday, December 16, 2015, Janus—"Hang on," I said to MJ. "My feet are cold. I need to get some socks." I left the phone on the bed and went to my dresser. When I pulled open my socks drawer, I found the present I'd planned to give Jackson for Christmas. I pulled the watch—a handmade, limited-edition Pioneer Basel Tourbillon—from its case. Removing it from its case started its delicate flying tourbillion in motion; the second hand began its precise sweep of the watch's rich blue face. Pulling the stem, I quickly set the time and wound the watch then slipped it onto my right wrist, despite the watch on my left wrist. I know I will wear it every day—otherwise, it will wind down. And that would feel like Jackson's heart stopping. Or perhaps my own.

"I'm back," I said picking up my phone.

"I just called to see how you were doing…"

"Jackson said I don't live in the moment," I blurted. "He says that I focus so much on tomorrow, on what's next, on who we'd be, that I miss the todays, the now, who we are. That I never rest. Presumably, Kitt lives in the present and doesn't think about what's next."

"She doesn't think about consequences either," MJ said darkly.

We fell silent for a few seconds, then MJ said, "He's right, you know. You *don't* live in the moment. You never rest."

So that was it? His unhappiness boiled down to that?

"Do you know why I don't live in the moment? Why I never rest?" I asked. "It's because so many of my moments growing up were crappy. The only way I could survive was to think about tomorrow—and how much better it would be. Then I met Jackson. I was so happy, so in love with him—I couldn't wait to experience what was next, the next day with him, the next year with him. I couldn't wait to find out who we'd be when we were old and gray and still together and in love. I wanted a lifetime with him. Can you understand that?"

"I can," she said gently.

And even after what Jackson and MJ said, I still find myself thinking about what I have to do next, tomorrow: admit to myself that this—Jackson and I—are over; sleep and begin picking up the pieces of myself; find a lawyer; sell our house; move.

LAVENDER (2016)

Thursday, January 28, 2016, Janus—I met with a lawyer today. It's official. I am divorcing Jackson. There doesn't seem to be anything else to do, and I must do *something*. We've been together thirty-nine years, married for one hundred and two days. I am Kim Kardashian. I am Britney Spears.

Quite frequently before the SCOTUS ruling, when the subject of marriage equality came up, often in heated arguments, I'd routinely dismissed all arguments by saying I didn't care because just as not being able to marry hadn't kept Jackson and I apart, getting married wouldn't keep us together. Now I feel myself choking on the very truth of those words.

Getting divorced is hard. Aside from the emotional cost, there is the financial cost. Under the terms of our divorce agreement, Jackson gets half of everything. We're selling our house, and he'll get half of that as well. I could easily have bought him out, but I can't bear the thought of living across the street from him and Kitt. My lawyer thinks I am being overly and unnecessarily generous. After all, he points out, I make more money than Jackson and have for a long time. I was the one who built then sold a successful business, the one who achieved. But even after everything that has happened, I can't bear the thought of Jackson in need, of him living in poverty. I just can't.

And while it's true I make more money than he does, that hasn't always been the case. When I was in college, Jackson often worked two jobs so I could be free to study. Even after I graduated and got a job and he got his plumber's license, he outearned me for years. And he took care of me. No matter how late I came home from work, he was there to ask how my day was and there was a warm meal on the table. If I had an important meeting, he made sure I had a pressed shirt to wear and matching socks. If I'd succeeded, if I'd soared, it was because of Jackson. He was the source of my power; he was the wind beneath my wings. Even now, outsiders looking at us may assume I am the hero in our story; no one ever seems to realize that *he* is *my* hero. And his is the only love I've ever known.

Sunday, March 15, 2016, Janus—"Upstairs or down?" the maître d' asked us. The restaurant, Milliways, is famous for its rotating dining room and its sheer glass walls; the upstairs restaurant, 700 feet above the ground, boasts a 360-degree view of the city below. It is as legendary for its view as it is for inducing motion sickness and vertigo in intrepid would-be diners as they shoot at high speed fifty stories up in a glass-walled elevator that climbs the side of the building in a transparent shaft. There are those who survive the elevator ride intact only to develop motion sickness once they are seated in the ceaselessly rotating dining room.

"Downstairs," I said before Claude could respond.

"I see," the maître d' said dismissively, branding us cowards despite Claude's outfit that was anything *but* cowardly, and directed us to the escalator behind him on his right.

As we stepped onto the escalator, Claude looked at me in surprise. "Are you afraid of heights?" she asked.

"No," I said. "I'm afraid of dying in an elevator traveling at the speed of light to an unnecessary height in pursuit of a forty-dollar cheeseburger."

She laughed.

The escalator delivered us to the second-floor iteration of the fabled fiftieth-floor dining room; this dining room was populated with the more timid and less pretentious, who recognized the ability to pay top dollar for food made from the finest and freshest ingredients and prepared by chefs trained in France and Italy, and served by stunning out-of-work actors and models, ought not to carry with it the threat of death by fire, mechanical failure, terrorism, or sheer fear.

I was surprised when Claude called and asked me to a late brunch—*just us*, she made a point of telling me. Now, I watched her carefully as she untucked her hands from her fur muff and laid it on the banquette beside her. Then she removed her matching hat and laid it on top of the muff.

"What would you like to drink?" our waiter asked.

"I'll have a French 75," Claude said.

"Very good, ma'am. And you, sir?"

"I'll have a negroni, please."

"What kind of gin?"

"Monkey 47."

Yes, sir."

The waiter placed our drinks on the table and took our brunch order. When he left, Claude reached for my hand. I guess our small talk and general pleasantries were about to end.

"We need to talk," she said. "Or rather I need to talk, and you need to listen. I just need to explain a decision Octavio and I have made and our reasoning. After, we can discuss. OK?"

I nodded and took a sip of my drink, nervous.

"Octavio and I have decided to remain in Jackson's life. I'm upset with him for hurting you. It was wrong and you deserve better. And I've told him that. If Mary Jane had a husband and she did to him what Jackson did to you, we would be so disappointed and angry, but we would not disown her. We consider you and Jackson as much a part of our family as Mary Jane. Nothing could make us stop loving any of you. You see, when Mary Jane promised to be your family, we became your family too. And without you, if Jackson didn't have us, who would he have?" Claude stopped talking abruptly. "Do you have any thoughts you'd like to share?" she asked.

"No. No. I mean, thank you for standing by Jackson—I hate the thought of him losing anyone else—and for telling me."

She reached for my hands again. She noticed the watch on my right hand, then glanced at the one on my left hand. "That's a beautiful watch," she said, gesturing to my right hand. "Do you always wear two?"

I shrugged. "It was the last watch I bought for Jackson. It was to be his Christmas present. He left before Christmas."

She raised an eyebrow.

"I know. I could have returned it, but somehow that felt like I was throwing him away…"

"You miss him, I take it?"

"How can I not? He's the love of my life."

"I know. You make it sound like it's over."

"Isn't it?"

"I'm not sure it is, Oren. You must understand, love is like matter in that it cannot be created or destroyed. It can only be transferred or converted from one form to another. And I *know* about matter. Before I was an interior designer, I was a high school physics teacher. That's why love so often turns to anger or hatred but doesn't just disappear. People talk about falling in love, and that usually means finding companionship with someone based on attraction and friendship, and yes, lust. But true love—love in its purest and rarest form—is preordained, and for those fortunate enough to experience it, falling in love for them is simply a recognition of something…an *inheriting of one's destiny*. Octavio and I are lucky enough to have that kind of love. Mary Jane isn't—though I don't think she misses it or even would want it. You and Jackson, though—you have that love Octavio and I have. It was obvious to me from the first time you and Jackson came to dinner."

Outside, as we waited for her Uber to arrive, she said, "I believe in your and Jackson's love, and I have no doubt you will find your way back to each other."

I smiled with what I thought was benign agreement, but she must have seen hopelessness instead, for she slipped her right hand from her muff and caressed my cheek. "My dear," she murmured, "you must believe, as I do."

Her Uber glided to the curb; I opened the door, and she slid inside with infinite grace. *Yass, Queen*, I thought. She slipped her hand into her muff to join its mate as I closed the door.

Watching me, she mouthed *I love you* through the closed window as the car pulled away.

Despite my apparent hopelessness, Jackson is still my first thought in the morning, and my last thought at night.

Tuesday, March 31, 2016, Janus—Leaving the lawyer's office this morning, Jackson and I ended up alone on the same elevator, which ran express to the lobby. During the elevator's descent, I asked, "Jackson, what happened?" It wasn't the first time I'd asked him that question.

"I love you," Jackson said, "but now I have to love someone else."

"It can't be that simple—"

"It *is* that simple. See, you—you—overcomplicate everything. You need a back story and a front story and rationality. *You need to make sense of things.*"

"I do."

"Things don't always make sense."

"Well, you're right there. I mean, you left me for a woman. *Kitt* of all women, for God's sake—"

"I didn't leave you for Kitt! Look, Oren, love isn't rational, and there isn't just one kind of love. It doesn't have to make sense. It's like the tide. It ebbs and flows. Sometimes it moves in unexpected directions."

"I don't understand any of this."

"Look, maybe I just want a new adventure. Maybe I want to write a new story—one for which I don't know the ending. Our story was written the day I asked you to stop pining over Rio and give me a chance to love you."

The elevator door opened, and he rushed out without saying goodbye, stopping only when he reached a corner of the lobby. I watched him bend over a planter; he appeared to be experiencing dry heaves.

Monday, April 20, 2016, Janus—This morning, blowing on my cup of microwaved freeze-dried coffee—try as I might, I cannot master Jackson's instructions—I stared out the window at Jackson cutting the grass across the wide street and expanses of lawn separating our—*my*—house from his and Kitt's.

I miss Jackson most in the morning, not just for his perfect coffee and our chocolate croissants. I miss waking up to feel him moving gently, insistently inside me while holding me so closely it felt like he was trying to get under my skin. I miss him.

Kitt emerged from the house, her blooming belly before her. They seemed to address each other in a tense exchange. I wanted to enjoy their apparent acrimony. I would have wished them both dead except that would leave their child an orphan, unloved. And having been unloved and without a family of my own, I did not have it in me to wish a similar fate on another unknown to me and born without malice or knowledge of me and what Blue Moon had meant to me. Eventually, Kitt went back in the house and Jackson continued cutting the grass, his back resolutely turned on our house and its overgrown lawn and unruly hedges. I made a mental note to look for a lawn service.

When I returned home tonight, the grass had been cut and the hedges trimmed. The lawn mower had been cleaned, and the gas can beside it filled. There was no other indication that Jackson had been here.

Saturday, April 30, 2016, Janus—"Take what you want," I told Jackson, not caring. "I've sold the house." In the end, he took nothing but clothes; his comic books; his dozen or so oversized "coffee table" books with their glossy photos and large font text, which I am sure will be a splendid addition to Kitt's half-dozen or so obscure feminist poetry collections; the collection of elegant timepieces—"They're too beautiful, too expensive to be called watches," he'd insisted—I'd created for him over nearly forty years; and his collection of stopped clocks. I wondered if he had one marking the precise time he'd decided to break my heart.

Kitt came with him, I suppose to keep him from jumping into bed with me, to keep him from admitting she had been a mistake, an aberration.

Jackson disappeared into our bedroom, leaving Kitt and I to stand in awkward silence, avoiding eye contact. She spoke first. "You didn't think I could do it, did you?"

"Do what?" I asked, hating her—this horsewoman of my personal apocalypse—more than I'd ever hated anyone; more than I hated my grandfather, more than I hated Reverend Jack.

"Pry Jackson from your grip." When I said nothing, she continued in that taunting way of hers, "It was surprisingly easy. I know you used you laugh at me."

"Well, your crush on Jackson seemed preposterous at the time."

Watching me, seeming to take my measure, she asked, "Know where you fucked up? You were always the hero—*his* hero. It never occurred to you that just once Jackson wanted to be *your* hero."

No one ever understands *he* is the one who saved *me*.

She continued, "*Every* man wants to feel like a hero, no matter how big a fuck-up he is."

Jackson reappeared. "I'm done. The movers will be here tomorrow?"

I nodded. "The estate agents will be here to prep for the sale on Friday the thirteenth. The sale is on the fourteenth and the fifteenth. Whatever doesn't sell, they will arrange to donate to Habitat for Humanity. The movers are scheduled for the seventeenth. Settlement is Thursday the nineteenth at ten."

"I'll be there—"

"*We'll* be there," Kitt said, taking his arm.

"No, not you," I said. "When Jackson and I started our life together, it was just the two of us. When we end it, I'd like it just to be the two of us."

Jackson shot her a look, silencing her. "*I'll* be there."

"Come on, Jack," Kitt said, tugging on his arm. I waited for Jackson's decades old retort: "*My name is Jackson, not Jack. Jack is my father.*" When he didn't say anything, I wondered if I'd known Jackson at all.

Saturday, May 7, 2016, Janus—"Hello, Sweetie," Perils said, hugging me. "I'm *so* sorry. I brought chocolate," she added, handing me a beribboned box with the logo of her family's restaurant emblazoned across the top. Perils is the CEO of her family's restaurant, and under her leadership, they have opened chocolate outposts in a few cities on the East Coast and are rumored to be opening other outposts in California.

"Are there any pralines in there?" MJ asked, edging around Perils to kiss my cheek.

MJ had pried Perils from the exurbs to come help me pack, though I suspected they were here more to check on me and lift my spirits.

"It doesn't look like he took much," MJ said, looking around.

"He only took some clothes, his three books, his clocks, and his watches," I told her.

Perils rocked back on her feet as if I'd dealt her a blow. "I told you about buying him watches! I told you time and again. Never buy a man a watch or shoes. If you do, you'll 'watch' him walk away—"

"What?" MJ interrupted. "Where'd you hear that? I've never heard such a ridiculous—"

"Terpe told me."

"Who's Terpe?" MJ asked like a detective stumbling on a clue, or more accurately, a news reporter sniffing out a false story.

Perils sighed dramatically. "I've told you before. Terpe was my mother's housekeeper when I was a kid, and she helped raise us. She was from the Virgin Islands and the smartest woman I've ever met."

Terpe's even wiser grandmother, a gifted obeah woman, had passed this dire warning on to her when she was eleven or twelve, Perils confided. MJ smiled indulgently at Perils, which Perils didn't appreciate. "Go ahead, laugh. My friend Mona didn't believe me either and she kept buying her husband shoes, even though I kept telling her not to."

"What happened?" I asked, getting sucked in despite myself.

"He died," Perils said, a hint of triumph in her voice.

What did you give to your husband? I wanted to ask Perils, she who had married and divorced the same man—a professional football player—twice. Instead, I said, "For forty years, I ate overcooked fish."

"What?" MJ and Perils asked in unison.

"Jackson always overcooked fish. He was afraid he'd get food poisoning unless the fish was ashes and cinder," I said.

"I know. That's why I never came over for dinner on Fridays," MJ said.

"For forty years, I ate overcooked fish," I repeated. "For us to end? Like this?"

It wasn't until I felt their arms around me that I realized I was crying.

"You know," MJ said when I'd stopped crying, "I've never wanted what you and Jackson had, as perfect as it was."

I knew she didn't. MJ is fiercely independent and essentially a loner. As she moved into her thirties and people would encourage her to find a husband, she would snap, "The only men I need permanently in my life are Oren and my father, possibly in that order."

"But," she continued, "you two breaking up has cut me to the bone."

"I know," Perils said, opening the box of chocolates. "It's as if the world started spinning in the opposite direction. It just doesn't seem possible."

"So, Jackson is straight now?" MJ asked.

"I don't think so," I answered slowly. "That's not how it works. Orientation isn't a sex act or lust. It's a pattern of attraction. And as far as I know, Jackson has never been attracted to women—any more than I."

"Then what happened? What *is* this?"

"I don't know. Jackson doesn't seem to know either—or at least, he can't explain it to me when I ask him to. He's never been good at communicating. It's the one thing that I found frustrating about him."

"I don't think Jackson is a bad communicator," MJ said tentatively. "You and I are excellent communicators, but then it's what we do for a living, isn't it? Also, you are far more articulate than Jackson. Back in school, whenever someone confused the two of you, DAX would say, 'Jackson is the pretty one. Oren is the articulate one.'"

Full of chocolate and having drunk the two bottles of Brachetto d'Acqui I'd found in the cold pantry, we set about the business of packing in earnest. We started in the kitchen, packing the cookbooks and French copper pots and the Foley mill and the citrus knife and the poultry shears and the lemon zesters and the steak knives.

Moving to the living room, as I handed them CDs, I thumbed through our collection, the soundtrack of our lives, the thrumming of our contentment: Michael Jackson; Prince; The Village People; Donna Summer; Grace Jones; Sugar Hill Gang; Aretha...

I'd already packed up the hundreds of books in the library. So next, we tackled the last of the dinner services: vintage Rosenthal China we'd bought at auction; maximalist Emma Shipley porcelain; sterling flatware we'd discovered at an estate sale. So many dishes, we'd converted the breezeway between the garage and the kitchen into a butler's pantry to house it all.

I emptied the art deco sideboards, reverently packing the napkin rings, tortoiseshell and alabaster and Bakelite, wondering at the life that had required such things. We'd hosted so many dinner parties, starting in college. I remember at the beginning, in our first apartment, MJ and Sue P and I cooking all day. And Perils would bring dessert and wine. Others would bring six-packs of beer. Once, someone brought an enormous watermelon cut in half and filled with sangria.

To participate, you only had to bring a cup, a plate, and a point of view—the entire party revolved around conversation. Word spread, and more and more people showed up each month: a friend would bring a friend, and that friend would bring a friend the next month. The party grew, spilling into the hallway of our building and eventually into the courtyard outside our apartment; food and drink and conversation were passed through the open windows.

"Earth to Oren. Calling Oren."

"Huh," I said, coming back myself.

"You were so far away. Where were you?" MJ asked with concern.

Lost in yesterday, and disgruntled to find myself in today, I wanted to answer but did not, shrugging instead and reaching for another packing crate.

Saturday, May 14, 2016, Janus—The first day of the estate sale was today. I was there against the advice of the estate agent running the sale. I assured her I'd be fine, wouldn't disclose who I was or change my mind about anything that was for sale. She relented. It was strange to see our house full of strangers— strangers sitting in our chairs to try them out, strangers touching our stuff, judging it, discounting its worth. One woman fondling a Basalt Ware bowl we'd found on an anniversary trip to Newport, asked *who would give this up?*

"Isn't it beautiful? And it's in perfect condition," one of the sales agents said brightly.

The woman looked at her, eyes wide. "Did the owners *die*?"

The estate agent looked around and, lowering her voice, confided, "Worse. They're getting *divorced*."

I left then. Sitting in the car at the end of our driveway, I wished Jackson had had the decency to die. My heart would have still been broken, but at least I wouldn't have been humiliated.

As a widower, I would be entitled to sympathy and casseroles. As it stood, *as the one cheated on*, I was greeted with pity and a certain suspicion: *Surely, you must have known. Surely, you had* some *idea.* Idea of what? That my neighbor and presumptive friend was pouring kerosene over my life and that my husband would strike the match that burned the life we'd built together to the ground?

"Forty isn't fatal," Linda Evans had famously said, and as it turned out, she was right; however, I wasn't sure being nearly sixty and suddenly single wasn't going to kill me.

Maybe I should have fought harder for Jackson. Maybe I should have tried *fucking* him, forcing him to remember he liked men. Except I've never been good at that. Only my tongue and my occasional finger had ever successfully ventured in his ass.

At least I can stop eating parsley and start taking vitamins, now that I no longer have to worry about the taste of my semen. I won't have to shave my underarms anymore. I'd first shaved on a lark back in college. Jackson had declared it dead sexy, so I'd kept it up. I wonder if the new Jackson finds Kitt's underarm hair sexy.

If Jackson had died, I wouldn't dream of him returning.

Tuesday, May 17, 2016, Janus—I walked through our house waiting for the movers to arrive, counting the boxes and crates, making sure they were all properly labeled. Again, I marveled at how far we'd come. When Jackson and I left Locust Hollow, we'd done so with just the clothes on our backs. And each other.

Next, I moved on to checking the closets and drawers to make sure nothing was left behind. At the back of a pantry drawer, I disentombed one of Jackson's old forgotten comic books. As I went to toss it in the trash, a letter fell out. It was from Jackson's mother. This one had been opened, so I pulled it out of the envelope and began to read it. She implied that my parents' descent into dipsomania was the result of willfulness, a weakness of character, self-indulgence, and warned Jackson apples don't fall far from their trees, pleading with him to abandon me before I dragged him into drunkenness and hell with me. She wrote as if my parents' drinking was the equivalent of giving head to the devil himself, unscrewing and drinking from the firehose of his depravity.

In the second half of the letter, she warned him that the sins of the father would be visited upon the son and urged him again to leave me, telling him I was truly calamitous, that my brothers were also my uncles.

The grotesqueness of the idea made me freeze. Surely, it wasn't true. Then I remembered my mother, how her smiles had slowly faded and the woman herself began to disintegrate. But what about my father? Why hadn't he protected her? And then I knew, *I just knew*. He couldn't protect himself from my grandfather's abuse; he couldn't protect his wife.

Their drinking then wasn't mere weakness but rather an attempt to cope with deep trauma and an inability to forget the unforgettable. The sin, the outrageousness, ended, the letter continued, the night my father pinned my grandfather's scrotum to the immaculate tongue-and-groove pine flooring in his bedroom with a Laguiole penknife that had a rosewood handle, the night she and my father died. State troopers had discovered him tacked to the floor, bleeding and semi-conscious, when they came to tell him his only daughter and son-in-law had perished. While planning their funeral, my grandfather had found Reverend Jack and Jesus—in that order—and confessed his sin, pledging to stomp out sin wherever he found it as penance.

Reading then re-reading her letter, I realized that the feminine handwriting may have been Jackson's mother's, but the words were not. Then this thought intruded: had my parents really intended to abandon us—*me*?

Thursday, May 19, 2016, Janus—Our house sold far more quickly than I anticipated. I would have moved even if it hadn't sold because I could no longer bear to live across the street from Jackson and...*her*. Kitt is probably due any day now, and I don't want to see Jackson pushing a stroller around the neighborhood. He will get half the proceeds per our divorce agreement. And then, because he refused to accept alimony, he and I will be done.

The pre-settlement walk-through for the buyers was scheduled for an hour before closing. I arrived early because I wanted to visit our house one last time. As I walked through the empty house to the front door, I glanced up at the portraits of the unknown matriarchs and patriarchs who seemed to stare down at me unhappily from their lofty perches; they may not have approved of Jackson and me, I imagined, but they were surely more dismayed at being left in an empty house, the suit of armor on its pedestal nestled into the curve of the main stair their only remaining company. I bid them a silent adieu and whispered

I'm sorry, the failure of my marriage rubbing against my shoulders like a hair shirt.

As I drove down the driveway for the last time, I glanced across the street at Kitt's house, I thought I glimpsed Jackson at the front window, watching me leave, shoulders quaking.

Saturday, June 18, 2016, St. Jude—Since our house sold, I'd been staying at Claude and Octavio's shore house. I think it did me good, the weeks with just sand between my toes, the limitless ocean filling my eyes, and my own thoughts dancing in my head. In the mornings and afternoons, I walked on the beach; in the evenings, I sat with sorrow—until my feet hurt and the sorrow faded.

Today, I moved into my new house—I can't think of it as home, not without Jackson in it. A low-slung modernist glass-enclosed rectangle, it is a far cry from our old house. The house seems to both cling to its fieldstone foundation *and* to soar above and free of it. It's as conflicted as I am.

A ribbon of narrow windows, high up, run along the front of the house on both sides of a massive unadorned blackened steel door, while at the back, an expanse of floor-to-ceiling windows in the living room and bedrooms face the back lawn, which terminates at the edge of the wide canal that runs behind all the houses here. Between the canal and the house stands a row of mature cherry blossom trees.

A trellised patio stretches across the entire back of the house, wrapping around the left side where it meets a high stone garden wall that shields it from the street. Mature Japanese wisteria, in full bloom, threads through the slats of the trellis, bathing the entire house in soothing lavender tones.

Older, plainer, and smaller than its swollen McMansion neighbors, it had sat on the market for 192 days. I felt an instant affinity with its undesired state. The house, pared down, low to the ground, and modern, was as foreign to its neighbors as my uncoupled state was to me. And so, we claimed each other, house and owner, two strangers in a strange land, a lavender mist dancing in the breeze around us.

Friday, June 24, 2016, St. Jude—Today marks thirty-nine years since Jackson and I graduated from high school. I'd always believed our love was a circle. With neither beginning nor ending, we could not escape; we could not be banished or separated. I thought all that last night as I tried to fall asleep in this silent new house, so far from home.

I remembered the first night Jackson and I spent together—the first night I'd ever felt safe at home. Now, I struggle to sleep without his arms around me. Jackson sleeps like a starfish: moving to the middle of the bed, arms thrown open, his legs spread wide. In defense, the only way to sleep with him was to curl myself around him. Capturing one leg between my thighs, I rested my head on his chest. His arms and legs during the night would fold around me, a starfish shrinking in the sun. Thus, we were able to share a bed for more than thirty-nine years.

Now I find myself alone, unable to sleep: a starfish on a beach too large with too much room and no sun to comfortably warm me, shrink me, wrap me up in love.

I've never lived alone before. I don't know how to stand without Jackson. If he was a desert, I was his ocean. If he was hungry, I was his daily bread. How had we become uncoupled?

I will, I know, learn to live without him, but at this moment, I don't want to. Until we'd moved in together, for me, home had always meant the sound of violence—chickens being slaughtered, days-old puppies being drowned, wood being chopped, doors slamming—the smell of blood, the gritty feel of dust.

Saturday, August 6, 2016, St. Jude—"What's taking so long?" MJ called impatiently from the living room. We were going to lunch then an early movie. MJ anchors Monday through Friday and often hosts her network's weekly news round-up on Sundays, so her free time is limited, and we try to do something together at least once a month, so I understood her impatience.

"I can't find anything to wear," I answered. "Every time I go to put something on, I discover Jackson took it."

"What?" MJ asked. She was standing in the doorway to my bedroom surveying the mess of clothes on the bed.

"Jackson took half of our clothes."

She snapped to attention. "Why would Jackson take half *your* clothes?"

"Well, they weren't really mine. I mean, we didn't have separate clothes. They were ours, but he took the stuff I like best."

MJ held up her hand; I fell silent. "Wait. You didn't have separate clothes?"

"Well, no. We wear the same size, and men's clothes don't have a lot of variety, so we just shared everything."

"Including underwear."

175

"Well, yeah. We shared pajamas too. I slept in the tops. He slept in the bottoms." Now, for the first time, I wondered if our sharing clothes was odd. Did other male couples not share a wardrobe?

"I've never heard of such a thing," MJ said.

I shrugged. "It's not like we had role models or a couple's roadmap to follow. We just did what felt right, making it up as we went along."

She shook her head and stared out the windows at the purple wisteria shivering in the breeze.

Monday, August 29, 2016, St. Jude—I quit my job today. I didn't plan to, I just did it. It occurred to me that I've spent the better part of my life climbing ladders and chasing coin. And the whole time, Jackson was coin of the realm.

I don't think I'll miss it—work, I mean. Though I didn't hate it—especially after I sold it and took on the role of founder emeritus, working only with the firm's biggest, most lucrative clients—it was not my love either. Jackson, like in most things, was the center of my work. He was the one I strove for, the one I wanted to do a little more for, to *achieve* for.

Jackson suffers from night terrors, which causes him to thrash about and scream in his sleep without waking. As I would try to comfort him, to still his twisting agony, he would stare at me, his eyes wide open but unseeing. He'd seem confused, lost, unsure who we were to each other, unable to place himself in the world. I, his North Star, his constant, would guide him back home. Now, I wondered if I'd been fair; what if he hadn't wanted to remember? What if Jackson wasn't who I thought he was? What if he didn't want to remain in the place he'd always wanted to be?

What if the heartbeat I heard in bed at night wasn't the answering rhythm to my own? What if he wanted to be somewhere else, *be someone else?*

In the morning, with no recollection of the terror, fear having passed like a fever, he'd pull me close, and we'd laugh and make love. But the questions would remain: what if where I wanted him to be, at my side, wasn't where he wanted to be?

It turned out to be true: he wanted to be somewhere else, to be someone else.

And here I sit like the North Star, cold and lonely in the arc of heaven with no earth to help me locate myself in the vast firmament. What use am I? What purpose do I serve? Can anyone even see me?

Tuesday, September 6, 2016, St. Jude—Jackson and I had been like two trees planted a foot apart leaning towards each other until we touched and, having touched, grew together until, finally, looking at them, you couldn't tell where one ended and the other began. Yet there came a braided lesbian Paul Bunyan carelessly wielding an axe, attempting to divide us into two, expecting us to survive despite our shared purpose, our shared heart. Jackson fell; I remained standing, alone, like that tree planted by the water, unsure, for the first time, that I could not be moved.

Alone. *What should I do to feel less alone? What should I do to find love?* I wonder. Dating apps are out of the question. I find myself questioning the wisdom of buying this house in St. Jude, a suburb, known as a "bedroom community" because the only thing to do here is sleep, fuck, and raise kids; the schools, they tell me, are excellent. Moving to the city, though, had seemed out of the question. I am too old for gay bars and clubs. When we were young and gay bars were an undreamed-of novelty, Jackson and I had gone but quickly abandoned the scene once we realized that it was safer—and *cheaper*—to dance and drink at home. Now, though, the cost of drinks isn't higher than the cost of being looked *over*, around, or not seen at all.

I find myself shrouded in a lavender mist, invisible unless you really looked, really wanted to see me.

Tuesday, October 11, 2016, St. Jude—Today is National Coming Out Day. And perhaps, not surprisingly, my birthday. No doubt to distract me from the sadness of my first birthday without Jackson, DAX asked me to join a panel discussion with a queer youth group that is part of his school's GSA, which he sponsors.

One kid, sort of timid with long hair and an unruly bang that obscured his eyes and which he constantly raked back only to have it fall over his eyes yet again—I named him Sisyphus—asked the panel when we first knew we were gay. The others answered; when it was my turn, I drew a breath, closed my eyes, and said, "His name was Rio. I'd always thought he was handsome, but one day after Christmas break—he was wearing this tight red shirt— I took one look at him, and I just *knew* I was gay and that I was in love with him."

When I opened my eyes, the students were staring at me. Even DAX looked curious.

"Did you to ever hook up?" Sisyphus asked; another kid, this one a girl with spiky hair dyed pink on one side and blue on the other, poked him in the ribs.

"It's a fine question," I said. "No. No, we never did. I didn't know him very well, even though I had this huge crush on him in high school. And anyway, he had a girlfriend—"

"What happened to him?"

"I don't know?"

Another student, quite androgynous in appearance, who introduced themselves as "Pepper, my pronouns are they/them," asked "Do you ever wonder what happened to him?"

"I do, actually."

"I bet you could find him on Facebook or something." Sisyphus said brightly.

We eventually moved on to other topics and questions, but on the drive home, I kept thinking about what Sisyphus said.

Rio had shown me who I was and what I wanted so that when Jackson finally found me, I was ready for him. I find myself wanting to tell Rio that.

Sisyphus's question, participating in that panel, talking about what was probably the most-defining moment of my life feels transformative. This exercise of memory and sharing has helped me to revisit a particular moment in time, to accurately describe the emotions of my fifteen-year-old self at what was a moment of discovery, a life-changing moment. I doubt he ever knew that I had a crush on him or that the simple act of him walking into homeroom after a winter's break, wearing a tight red knit shirt, caused me to see myself in a different light. Without meaning to, he'd shown me a door, and I'd chosen, in that instant, to step through. I've never looked back at what could have been but wasn't meant to be. Who I am now is who I needed to be. Still, I wonder where Rio is now. I want to find him, I've decided, and tell him how he, without meaning to, or even knowing it, changed my life.

Wednesday, November 16, 2016, St. Jude—It came today—our divorce decree. I stared at the words bolded in a hideous serif font on creamy cotton bond paper: Petition for Dissolution of Marriage. And just like that, our marriage and everything we had been to each other...*dissolved.*

I stared at the paper filled to the narrow margins with unintelligible legalese and the occasional Latin-looking phrase. And just like that, it was over. Just like that, I found myself, as my grandmother would have said, back on the market again. And like a dollar saved for a rainy day, I found myself in a rainy season, unsure if the currency I had was enough to buy what I desperately needed.

RED, BLACK & YELLOW (2017)

Wednesday, January 25, 2017, St. Jude—It's been a month since Rio and I reconnected. I found him on Christmas Day, which is also his birthday. It was surprisingly easy to find him. (Thanks, Facebook!) We've been talking or messaging each other daily. He's very easy to talk to. We love catching up, learning about each other. In a way, it reminds me of the early days of Jackson's and my courtship.

He seems touched that I had thought him handsome, that I'd had a crush on him, had tried to imagine a life with him. "You should have told me back then," he said. "Who knows what might have happened?" he teasingly added.

Of course, he'd heard the gossip about me and Jackson, but he hadn't believed it. "You were too innocent, and Jackson was the preacher's kid. Besides, back then, I couldn't imagine two guys in love with each other."

"And now?" I asked.

"Now, it's kind of cool. It's kinda sexy to imagine. And I love knowing you were in love with me."

Rio was raised by his grandparents, like a lot of us in Locust Hollow, because a generation, Reverend Jack proclaimed with a kind of mournful glee, were seduced, had succumbed, and been lost to the devil's syncopated rhythms of sex, drugs, and rock 'n' roll.

"My grandparents resented having to raise me and they weren't really kind to me. And they *hated* spending money on me," Rio told me. "So, I didn't have many clothes, and sometimes I would wear the same clothes for two or three days in a row. The kids would point at me and chant, 'Repeats! Repeats.' You never did, though, and I remember you always shared your art supplies with me when I didn't have my own."

Up until freshman year of high school, we'd maintained a friendship of sorts. Then puberty found him, earlier than the rest of us, and he'd shot up a foot, his voice deepened, his shoulders broadened. In short, he got hot. All the girls wanted to date him, and all the guys wanted to hang around him. I got left behind with other childish things.

"You were always so quiet. You were always alone, always carrying a book. I remember the books you carried most because whenever we split up into teams, no one would pick you, or they'd send you where you couldn't do any harm. You'd just go off and read your book."

Being as popular as he was and athletic, Rio was always named team captain and as such got to choose his players first. And always his team was the "skins" in games of "shirts vs. skins." I can still see him pulling his T-shirt over his head, revealing his taut, flat belly and the treasure trail that snaked down into his shorts. I did not remind him that he had never chosen me for his team. Not once. I remember the day I'd finally had enough and kicked Lidell in the balls; Rio had looked me right in the eyes, as he often did, and chosen someone else. Over and over again until I was the last boy left and by default placed on his opposing team. I did not remind him of this.

Rio attended State College in a lush green valley on the other side of the mountains—the same one Mr. Fabricant had encouraged me to apply to. I had had no intention of going to a school so close to Locust Hollow, so close my grandfather could easily grab me with his callused, cruel hands, and plunk me back into the dust and ashes that had been my world since I was seven years old; I hadn't even applied for admission, not even as my "safety school."

Rio became a music teacher, returning to our old high school to teach after Miss Miller retired. He'd soon grown bored with teaching, though, and with Mr. Fabricant's help and encouragement, he'd gone on to grad school then worked as a music therapist. When he got bored with that, he'd set out for LA to start a career in music. Once there, he started writing and producing pop and R&B songs. He had a number of hits but grew increasingly disillusioned with the music business and eventually left it, too. Next, he set out on a tour of Europe, working odd jobs and staying in youth hostels. Now he thinks he wants to be a poet, maybe write a children's book. He appears to live off his modest royalty income.

Saturday, February 11, 2017, St. Jude—Every conversation with Rio is like reading a new chapter in a mystery novel—I get closer to solving the puzzle of Rio, the boy I thought I loved in high school. He lives with his ex-wife, or rather in his ex-wife's basement, though this arrangement seems to provide him less with a home than a place to touch down between adventures, a launch pad to his next exploit. "I never stay long," he told me. "There's too much chaos and buckshot."

"What do you mean?" I asked.

"Vi," Rio said, "is bipolar. She is the wife who shouldn't have been. Our marriage should never have been."

"Was she always like this?" I asked.

"No, not until we got married. Putting a ring on her finger was like unlocking the raging lunatic inside. Have I told you how glad I am you found me?" Rios asked abruptly.

"I'm glad I found you, too," I said.

"I'll never forget it was Christmas Day, and I was so down because Vi didn't even remember it was my birthday, and there was no one in my life to share it with."

"I'm sorry. But I'm here now."

"Yes, here in my heart," he said.

Tuesday, February 28, 2017

Rio: How are you, babe? I'm very tired.

Oren: I'm good. Why tired?

Rio: Vi was in a rage last night. I still don't know over what. I'm still sweeping up broken dishes and glasses in the kitchen.

Oren: I'm so sorry.

Rio: It's OK. She'll settle down soon. That she was so angry, so emotional, means she's coming out of her depressive state and can feel again.

Oren: Oh. That's good. I guess?

Rio: Yeah. Unless she goes into a manic episode, in which case, she'll probably buy a car she can't afford or put the house on the market again.

Oren: She seems like she's a lot.

Rio: She is. It helps to have you to talk to. OK, gotta go finish cleaning up this mess. Talk later.

Oren: OK. Later.

Wednesday, March 15, 2017, St. Jude—This morning Rio called me. "Hey, babe" he said. "I dreamt about you last night."

Babe. He calls me that. A term of endearment, I know. I wonder at this. Jackson and I never used terms of endearment. I think just being able to rely on each other, to be able to call out each other's name in passion or need, made our names sacred. Our names were a prayer of love on our lips; we hadn't needed endearments.

"Oh," I said, slightly surprised. "Was it a good dream?"

"Yes," he said. "Very good. I dreamt…I was inside you…"

"Did you…ummm…like it?"

"Check your text messages."

When I looked at my phone, I discovered he'd texted me a picture: a black jockstrap was pulled aside to reveal an erect penis. His, I presumed. It was impressive, jutting out of a thicket of unruly pubic hair.

"You like?"

"I like," I said as Roscoe stirred in my underwear. Roscoe! Early on, in a playful mood, Jackson had named my dick Roscoe. I've no idea why. And I hadn't thought of this in years.

"Hello?" Rio said in my ear as my worlds collided—the world of Jackson and the world of Rio.

"Hi. *Hello.* I'm here. Sorry, I was distracted by this picture."

Can I tell you something?"

"Of course. You can tell me anything."

"I've never thought about having sex with a guy before…"

"And now?"

"Now, I can't *stop* thinking about it—except you're the only guy I can imagine being intimate with."

I didn't know what to say, couldn't stop smiling into the phone.

"Hello?" You there?"

"I'm here."

"OK, I gotta go. I just wanted you to know that in case I get run over by a bus or something."

I don't expect this absurd flirtation with Rio to go anywhere, but it does help me to think about Jackson less. And then there's the romantic allure of developing a relationship with your secret high school crush decades after the fact.

I suppose Rio is seducing me less with the promise of sex than the promise of romance, of a dream coming true, of a second chance, of love after the apocalypse.

Monday, March 20, 2017

Rio: Where are you, babe? I've been messaging you all morning.

Oren: Sorry. I had a colonoscopy scheduled for this morning.

Rio: Everything OK?

Oren: Yeah. Precautionary. I was having some issues with bleeding. Turns out I'm fine.

Rio: You got your results already?

Oren: Yeah. Dr gave me results as soon as I woke up. I got a WRITTEN report—with the most appalling photos. LOL

Rio: Of your asshole? Or your ass's interior?

Oren: Interior. Worse, there were *eight* people in the room when they put me under. All of them there presumably to look up my butt.

Rio: Well, I know you like an audience…

Oren: Ha-ha. I told them I was excited to see so many people turn out to view my innards. They actually applauded. It was hilarious…

Rio: You're too funny. I'm glad all is good in the Oren nether regions.

Oren: LOL. So am I. I'm relieved actually.

Rio: Me, too. I just found you. I don't want to lose you.

Oren: You won't. I'm not going anywhere. We have a lot to do. Plus, we still need to meet in person.

Saturday, April 1, 2017

Rio: Can I ask you a question?

Oren: Of course. I keep telling you, you can ask me anything.

Rio: Have you ever been back to Locust Hollow?

Oren: No. Why on earth would I do that?

Rio: Would you go if I asked you to?

Oren: What's going on?

Rio: Our 40th reunion is in June and I'm going. I'll be staying with Mr. Fabricant for a few weeks. I need to get away from Vi for a bit. Mr. Fabricant is taking a cross-country trip and will be gone most of the summer. He's letting me stay at his house for free in exchange for watering his plants and cutting the grass.

Oren: Is everything in his house still wrapped in plastic?

Rio: Yes. But it's clean and quiet. I could use some peace.

Oren: I bet.

Rio: So, I was thinking it would be really nice if we could finally meet in person.

Oren: You want to meet in person?

Rio: Yeah. Don't you? I love our chats, but I really, really want to see you.

Oren: OK.

Rio: OK, what?

Oren: OK. I'll go.

Rio: YIPPEE.

Friday, June 2, 2017

Oren: I saw your Facebook post from yesterday. You OK?

Rio: Yeah. Some asshole hit my car.

Oren: That sucks. Assholes are everywhere. How's the car?

Rio: My Subaru is a tank. But the bumper and headlights need to be replaced.

Oren: I know money is tight so let me know if you need me to cover the cost of repairs.

Rio: I'm touched by your offer, but the asshole's insurance is covering it.

Oren: OK.

Rio: I'm not used to anyone caring for me.

Oren: You'll get used to it.

Rio: I have to go. I have to take my car in to get the damage appraised. Love you...

Oren: K. Later.

Thursday, June 15, 2017

Rio: Hey! I just got my car back, so I'm gonna drive down to Locust Hollow tonight.

Oren: OK. Travel safe.

Rio: I'll see you at the reunion still, right?

Oren: I'll be there. But only because of you.

Rio: 😎

Saturday, June 17, 2017, Locust Hollow—There it was: the exit ramp to Locust Hollow. My jaw had been clenched for the last hour, and now my stomach was clenching, too. Only Rio could have gotten me to return here. Only my life falling apart could have brought me back here where it all began in such ugliness.

The first thing I noticed once I exited was the oily smoothness of the road. Farther on towards town, where fields of wheat and corn had once lain, were now neat houses swollen with square footage and self-importance, fronted by sweeping preternaturally green lawns and flanked by columns and porticos, upper stories boasting Juliet balconies and capped by cupolas and widow's walks.

The hollowed-out shell of downtown where Jackson and I had roamed so freely has been sketched in as if with a gentrifying Etch-A-Sketch: there is a Starbucks, a Whole Foods, a W hotel. At the end of the horseshoe-shaped Main Street, the old slaughterhouse still stands, though it's been converted into an event space. Rio told me Mr. Fabricant was a half-owner, which perhaps explained its name: *Abattoir.* But everyone still called it "The Bucket of Blood."

I turned into the small parking lot and immediately felt self-conscious as I guided my Range Rover into a spot between an old Honda sedan that was mostly rust and an ancient Subaru Baja, battered but still bright, yellow with a red-and-black pinstripe, vivid as a scar, that wrapped around it.

Twilight was settling as I mounted the stairs; my attention was snagged by the circling buzzards, who had apparently been lured by the folklore of the plentiful slaughterhouse offal that had been daily swept into the river at high tide back in the day. Drawing a breath, I opened the door. Inside, it was hot and crowded. With each reluctant step I took, sawdust, which covered the floor, rose to mix with cigarette smoke and the cloying smell of Elizabeth Taylor's White Diamonds perfume. Paper streamers—purple and white—our school colors—hanging from the low ceiling tickled my shoulders.

In the middle of the vestibule stood a table with neatly printed name badges in plastic shields laid on it in alphabetical order. Behind the table was Lidell Holloway, paunchy and middle-aged. I looked at him, this cliché: the teen athlete gone to seed. A bully on and off the field, he'd prayed the loudest over Jackson and me and laid his hands on us the heaviest.

"Is that you? O Strange One?" Lidell asked loudly, familiarity in his tone, as if we'd been pals, the nickname itself, which he'd thought such a clever play on my name, anathema to my ears.

I ignored the hand he extended to me and, pretending to look for my name badge, asked, "I'm sorry, do I know you?" He stormed off muttering as I picked up my name tag. I stepped away from the table and smack into the Lidell's mother, Lurene.

"Oren! Why Oren Strange! We never expected to see you 'round these parts ever again. You left so abruptly, and then, well, you know, we heard about so many young men like you...lost ...we thought..." She trailed off.

"You thought what?" I asked, not giving her an inch. I knew what she'd—*what they'd all* probably thought. A few years after we'd left University City, the country had been caught up in the pandemic that no one seemed to understand. Its name kept changing—gay cancer, GRID, AIDS—as if not only did no one understand it or know how to stop or at least slow the disease's rampant spread, they couldn't even decide what to call it. Perhaps because it was only affecting gay men, they didn't care. And while the pandemic had touched us early on, it had been at a distance, for Jackson and I were too poor, too dark, too attached to each other to be pulled into the maelstrom.

At first, we'd remained apart, touched, aggrieved, and unseen. By dint of unpopularity—or maybe it was something else—we remained safe, just out of reach of the disease. But we saw them, *the touched*, everywhere—men in their twenties and thirties tattooed with blue circles of doom, skinny and desperate as heroin addicts, moving unsteadily and with great effort as if weighed down by four score and seven years of pain. We saw the way others looked at us, avoided shaking our hands, assuming we too were afflicted. Jackson and I had clung to each other more tightly. We were terrified. We were all we had; if something happened to one of us, the other would have been lost.

Later on, we'd started to lose the gay men in our lives, men who we saw at our monthly dinner parties, men who'd sat across the table from us sharing food and conversation. They'd begun dying here and there one by one, then more frequently and in greater numbers until our dining room was empty and we felt as if we'd moved to a foreign land where we knew no one.

"Well, never mind all that," Lurene said with renewed vigor. "Oh! Look, here comes Fontella Bass—you remember her. She worked at the bank."

I turned to see Fontella barreling towards me. Having evidently traded the glamour of bank telling and prophecy making for waitressing, she rushed at me, a tray of canapés in front of her; she wielded the tray like a shield.

"You're back. I *knew* you'd be back!" she announced triumphantly. Nothing like a prophecy fulfilled, I suppose. "Bet you wish you'd kept that bank account open like I told you to!"

"This is my first time back in forty years—"

"Yeah, but you back, ain't you?" she asked and withdrew with her tray of canapés before I could snap, "I'm not staying."

I regretted coming already. Had my life not recently fallen, unexpectedly, apart, I wouldn't have come to this reunion. And Rio had asked me to. I'd come wanting to see him, needing to *see* him after all these years. Now that he was across the room from me, I was frozen. *What had I been thinking?*

Then, a rumble of laughter. Like echoes of thunder up at the quarry, it went on and on; it was the most absurd and welcome sound in the world, for it told me Rio had already arrived. I looked for him but could not see him, but his laugh had erupted from a gaggle of women gathered in a circle. I assumed he was their center.

Fontella suddenly reappeared with her tray of canapés. "We saw your old 'friend' a few months back—"

"What old friend?" I asked, irritated by the euphemism for what Jackson had been to me, what we'd been to each other.

"The one you always ran about with. Jack—the reverend's son."

"Jackson. His name is Jackson. Jack was his father, the reverend."

She looked at me perplexed, then nonplussed, continued, "He was here for his mother's funeral."

His mother died? I wondered as she paused.

"It was the darndest thing. He planned the whole thing long distance then showed up the day of the funeral. You've never seen so many different flowers, each bouquet more beautiful than the last. And the music—heaven! He said he wanted his mother in her death to have all the beauty she didn't have in life. Ain't that just the darndest thing to say? Then he gave the reverend's house and everything in it to the church—all legal like, too. And he never stepped foot in it, not once, when he came back. Said he was through being a preacher's kid, that it had cost him everything. Ain't that just the darndest thing you ever heard?"

When I didn't respond, she looked at me as if she'd forgotten I was there, that she'd been talking to me.

"I never understood why *you* never came back," Fontella said, recapturing my attention. "Not when Reverend Jack died, not when your grandpa died—God rest their souls—not when your brothers got convicted and sent up to Graterford. It's not like anyone here ever bullied you or anything..."

Did she really think that ostracizing me, whispering about me and Jackson, laying their hands on us Sunday after Sunday was a form of welcome? I was about to ask this when there was a tap on my shoulder. I turned around to find Rio standing in front of me.

"Hi," he said, taking my arm and leading me away. "You looked like you needed rescuing."

I stared at him, mute. I knew what I wanted to say to him—had rehearsed my opening gambit, what would follow. My thoughts now, though, diaphanous as chiffon, were disordered.

His post-puberty mustache was now a full-blown beard. He had broadened and thickened with age. His clothes fit him a little too snugly, as if he felt not buying larger clothes would mean he hadn't gained weight, or as if he planned to start a diet on a tomorrow that never seemed to come. He walked with a slight limp, the result of a hip in need of replacement—*but the doctor says I'm too young*, he'd explained—so he used a walking stick. Imagining the bulk of him on top of me, I found him sexier now than I had in high school. I unexpectedly found myself trying to tamp down my desire.

"Hey," he said. "You look the same."

When I simply nodded, he grabbed my arm and steered me to the bar and ordered two dirty martinis with extra olives.

"That's not on the menu," the bartender, a girl with messy hair and too much makeup, said.

"Can't you make an exception for me?" Rio asked. "Pretty please?"

"Well…" she said as if she was unsure. Meanwhile, I was sure—sure that I'd catch a chill from the breeze created by the furious batting of her false eyelashes that sat below her drawn-on eyebrows like twin tarantulas. I looked over at the food table covered with trays of Ritz crackers, cubes of Cracker Barrel cheese, pimento-stuffed olives, and imitation crab dip.

"OK, I guess I could," she said finally. "For you."

"You're a sweetheart," Rio said, glancing at me. I took the hint and placed a folded twenty-dollar bill in her tip jar.

"Don't be like that," Rio said, handing me a glass and steering me to an empty table in the corner.

"Be like what?" I asked, perplexed.

"Jealous that she was flirting with me." He laughed. "It got us decent drinks. Who actually drinks Rolling Rock?"

"Oh," I said and took a greedy sip of my martini as if it was Alice's found elixir and would shrink me so I could escape down the nearest rabbit hole.

I had thought I would stay over, perhaps at the new W, but now I just wanted to escape Rio's unexpected affection and wash off the stench of unfulfilled promise and cigarette smoke and Elizabeth Taylor's White Diamonds. When I broke the news that

I was leaving, Rio insisted on walking me to my car. When we got to where I'd parked, he said, "You parked next to me. That's probably the universe telling us we belong together."

Rattled, I asked, "Which car is yours?"

"The Subaru," he said.

I got into my car, started the engine and rolled down the window, prepared to say goodbye. Rio settled his arms on the doorframe and leaned in so close I could feel his breath. "What do you think?" he asked.

"About what?"

"Me, silly."

"What about you?"

"I've changed, I know. I'm older, I have a bad hip. Do you still think I'm handsome? Are you still attracted to me?"

Is he flirting with me? I wondered. He seemed genuinely curious, concerned even. "Yes," I said as casually as I could, "I still think you're handsome. And yep, I still have the hots for you." It was true. The intensity of my desire for him had startled me.

"But I look different."

I shrugged in the dark. "You're still you. You're like a beloved vase that one day falls and breaks. You glue it back together. And you still love it and think it's beautiful, even with that scar of glue. You know it's been through something, but it's still there with you and bringing you joy."

"I wish you would…"

"Would what?"

"Let me bring you joy."

When I said nothing, he nodded as if agreeing with something he heard in his head or in my silence. His brilliant teeth flashed white in the dark. "If you change your mind about staying," he said, "I'll be spending the night at Mr. Fabricant's. You know where his house is."

I recalled all of this as I stepped out of the shower in my suite at Locust Hollow's brand-new W hotel, exhausted from the drive, from the reunion, from seeing Rio and the resurgence of desire. I regarded my reflection. My pubic hair, once a dark forest, is now an iron-colored thicket. When had that happened and why had I not noticed? I wondered.

I sucked in my stomach and tried to see the abs I'd never had. Moving to the full-length mirror behind the bathroom door, I examined myself from every possible angle: my butt was still high and firm, slightly bubbled; my legs, from behind my knees to my ankles, were still mottled, the lasting reminder of eczema; I was speckled as a hen.

I've never been naked in front of any man but Jackson. What if my rendezvous with Rio ended up with us in bed together? Frightened by the idea, I pulled on a T-shirt and turned out the light. In bed, I tried to fall asleep, but Rio kept dancing at the edges of my vision, peeping under the covers at me, his hands dragging curiously over my body.

I worried also in this time of equality and versatility, that I was an anachronism: I wasn't a top. Jackson and I had tried once or twice; he'd gritted his teeth and tried to bear me entering him. I'd felt as a man, I should suck it up and deliver what he wanted. In truth, I hated topping; it pinched. Fortunately, one night before things went too far, we'd talked and, to our mutual relief, decided that wasn't something either of us wanted. But what if Rio expected to flip-flop—something I'd noticed, appalled, in porn? What if I was too set in my ways, too old to learn this new trick?

Sleeping with Rio, once an impossible thing, now loomed as a possibility, so the idea that there might be an expectation on his part, out of curiosity, to be topped did not seem out of the question.

Wednesday, July 5, 2017, St. Jude—Today, Rio texted me a picture of him from the waist down, sitting in pajama bottoms in a red-and-black plaid with a yellow stripe running through them. I texted, "I'm jealous." And I was. Here it was noon, and he was just waking up while I'd been unable to sleep last night; I'd finally given up and crawled out of bed, defeated, at five a.m.

"Of my hand?" he texted back. It was only then that I realized in the picture his hand was shoved down the front of his pants.

He immediately sent another photo, this one with his pants lowered; his thickening penis emerging from his tangle of unruly pubic hair, lay across his palm semi-hard, the red, black, and yellow flannel now bunched under his balls.

"Thinking of me?" I texted, feeling bold.

"I dreamed of you again," he texted back. "Would you really like to feel me inside you?"

Yes. A thousand times yes, I wanted to shout.

Monday, September 18, 2017, St. Jude—"Hey, Rio," I said answering my phone. I was surprised by the call. We haven't spoken much in the last couple of months. Assuming he needed time and space to figure out what was happening between us, I hadn't reached out much. Now he sounded like his old self.

"Hey, babe," he said, picking up right where he'd left off as if we hadn't gone months without contact. "I wanted to call because I saw the photos you posted on Facebook last night.

I'd gone with MJ to yet another awards dinner and posted photos to give her a boost. Her marketing team loved when I did that.

"You looked so handsome and sexy all dressed up." He stopped talking abruptly.

"Rio? You still there?"

"I'm here," he said after another pause. "I just can't believe I just told a guy he looked handsome and sexy."

"Well, if it's any consolation, I can't believe my straight high school crush just told me I looked sexy. Every time I talk to you, I wonder if I'm dreaming. Or if maybe, we've fallen into some alternate universe..."

"Maybe," he agreed. "But the thing is, I mean it. But I've never, *ever* looked at another guy and thought he was sexy. I wanted to like your post, but I was sure if I did, everyone would know what I was thinking."

Now it was my turn to fall silent.

"So," Rio said changing the subject, "how did you get invited?"

"Mary Jane invited me. She doesn't really date, so I'm often her plus-one. When Jackson and I were together, we were often her plus-two. People were *very* confused."

"You *know* Mary Jane Mitchell?"

"MJ? Yeah. We went to college together."

"So, she was friends with Jackson, too?"

"Of course she was. He and I were already together when she and I met freshman year."

"Do you think she'd like me?"

"She's my best friend. She loves me. I probably love you, so of course she'd like you."

He seemed satisfied with that answer for a moment then said, "I thought *I* was your best friend."

"My best friend? No, Rio. You are something altogether different."

"I am? What am I then?"

"I...don't know. I honestly don't..."

And I don't. But I know I don't want him to stop being whatever it is he is to me.

PINK (2018)

January 31, 2018

Rio: Hey, can I ask you something? You busy right now?

Oren: Of course. I keep telling you, you can ask me anything.

Rio: Do you ever fantasize about me?

Oren: OMG. Yes. Sorry. Why?

Rio: LOL

Rio: Because I was hoping you did. I'm glad you do. I fantasize about you too.

Rio: I sometimes think of you sucking my cock.

Rio: Is that what you think of?

Rio: Don't be shy now...

Rio: Hello???

Oren: Sorry. Yes, I'd love to suck your dick.

Oren: And I want to feel your dick inside me. I have a boner just typing this.

Rio: LOL. Sorry to be the cause of that.

Rio: And I want you to know I've visualized myself fucking you too.

Oren: I love that you visualize that.

Rio: And I think you're the only male I would ever allow myself to do that with because of how I love you and our connection.

Rio: It's really interesting. And a big turn-on.

Rio: There you have it. I figured you should know that before we died. LOL

Oren: God, I love you. I love that I'm the only man you can think of doing that with.

Rio: Loving you back!!

Tuesday, February 27, 2017, St. Jude—Rio messaged me this morning and told me he's in Spain, sharing a house and a bed with a female "friend" whose bed happened to be empty. When I asked why, he texted back: "I couldn't spend another minute with Vi." He doesn't know when he'll return—he bought a one-way ticket. He seems like a nomad. The total opposite of me. Once I'd torn myself from the dirt of Locust Hollow, I'd wanted only to put down again my jagged roots.

I am surprised by how hurt I am by his news. I'd thought we were on the verge of something. I wanted to ask him why he hadn't asked me to go with him, why he didn't come here? *Stop it*, I chided myself; I know I'm acting like I'm still that lovesick teenager pining for Rio. Except then he'd been two desks away and now he's more than halfway across the world sharing some woman's bed on a whim. Still, he *had* asked me, "do you ever fantasize about me?" Though he'd asked the question via text, I could hear it asked in that deep voice of his that had remained unchanged since puberty.

March 27, 2017

Rio: I'm baaack.

Oren: When did you get back?

Rio: Last night.

Rio: Did you miss me?

Rio: ??

Sunday, April 1, 2017, St. Jude—It's Easter Sunday today. This morning, I awoke to a text from Rio. When I turned over my phone, I saw he had sent me the cutest picture. It was of him, naked in bed except for on his head, which was propped up by his pillows, he wore a pair of pink fuzzy rabbit ears, and a collection of brightly colored plastic Easter eggs covered his crotch. "Happy Easter," he wrote underneath.

Before I could respond, he sent another text, this one a close-up of his erection poking through the Easter eggs at his crotch. Underneath, he'd written with appalling irreverence, "He is risen."

Rolling onto my stomach and pressing my erection into the mattress, I texted back, "He is risen, indeed!" Then, "What prompted that?"

"Lying here…thinking of you," he texted back.

I rolled onto my back, luxuriating in the feel of my erection and the warmth of his lust. "Really?"

"Yes really, silly. I told you…I love you."

Pondering his words and wondering how to respond, his incoming text broke my thoughts. "I hear Vi stomping around upstairs. I have to go. Text you later."

Vi. Why are there so many women in his life?

April 20, 2017

Rio: Hey. Sorry I've been out of touch. Been busy.

Oren: You working on something? New music?

Rio: No. I want to take a break from music. I want to write a children's book.

Oren: Oh…

Rio: I think you can help.

Oren: Sure. I have contacts—graphic designers, artists—who could help with stuff like illustrations, cover design, and such.

Rio: No, I meant you could help me write it.

Oren: I'm not a writer.

Rio: Modest. I read your LinkedIn profile. It says you're a storyteller.

Oren: I helped global companies tell their stories to employees, customers, and investors to reduce attrition, build brand loyalty, and keep investors invested enough to not run at the first dip in earnings. That's not the same thing as writing a book.

Rio: If you could tell a story to do all that, you can certainly help write a children's book.

Oren: LOL. What would it be about?

Rio: Music. I'm thinking two clefs meet, a treble clef and a bass clef, and fall in love and decide they could make beautiful music together, so they create concertos and operas. I see the front cover with the two symbols embracing, which would form a heart...

Oren: Nice!

Rio: It could be a metaphor for us.

Oren: Oh. You've thought about this?

Rio: Sorry, I have to go. I hear Vi coming downstairs. She never comes down here. This can't be good.

Oren: OK, text me later. Stay safe.

April 29, 2018

Rio: Hey.

Oren: Hey. What are you up to? How's the book coming?

Rio: I haven't started writing it yet. It's too chaotic and toxic here. Maybe if I crashed with you for a few weeks, we could start something??!! LOL

Oren: Start something? You mean your children's book, right?

Rio: Yes. Though, you never know what else might happen?!

Oren: You're such a tease!

Rio: Maybe I'm not teasing. It's been a long time since I last had sex. LOL. And I keep looking at that picture of you and MJ at that awards dinner. You look so dapper and damned sexy!

Oren: Hmmm. Well, you know I'd like to help...

Oren: And I know how that feels. I haven't had sex since Jackson left.

Rio: Vi is selling the house, so I have to get out. Do you have a couch I can crash on next month for a couple of weeks??!!

Oren: Better. I have an entire guest suite with its own bathroom and balcony.

Rio: What, I'm not welcome in the master bedroom?

Oren: You asked for a couch!

Wednesday, May 9, 2018, St. Jude—Hearing the crunch of gravel, I looked out the window to see Rio coming down the driveway in his ancient bright-yellow Subaru Baja with its red-and-black pinstripe along the sides. I walked outside to help him with his bags and was surprised by how little he had. After an awkward hug (just the feel of his arms around me was enough to wake Roscoe from his slumber), I led him to the guest room to put his things down. Then we retreated to the den. Beyond the windows, the clean, clear canal glittered like shards of mirror reflecting pink flowers on the cherry blossom trees, suffusing the room with a warm, rosy light.

Turning from the windows, he looked around the room curiously. Dotted around the room, often in clusters of three, were crystal vases filled with rocks. Picking one up and examining it, he asked, "Rocks? Why rocks?"

I shrugged, slightly embarrassed. "I think they're beautiful. I like that thousands of people, longing for beauty but not expecting to find beauty, unwilling to look for it, assume it isn't there and so walk right past it."

"But why not flowers?"

"Flowers wither and die. I like permanence. I suppose that's why I've never had a one-night stand or a hookup…"

"You've never—"

I shook my head. "I'm too romantic, I suppose. Besides, Jackson and I were together since we were sixteen years old."

"I love that about you—you're loyal and a romantic," he said.

Love. There was that word again. I busied myself at the bar. "Martini, right?" I asked.

"Yes, very dirty."

"Is there any other kind?" I handed him his martini.

"To us?" he asked, lightly. We clinked glasses. I hadn't been this nervous since the first time I'd visited Jackson in his bedroom in his parents' absence.

The sun was setting, coloring the room a deeper rose then eventually flooding it with dense pink light. I'd lost track of how many drinks we'd had; the charcuterie tray on the table in front of us held just some crumbs, a handful of deep purple grapes, and the rind of a cheese wheel.

I was thinking I should get up and start dinner for us, when Rio suddenly asked, "Do you…do you still *like* me?"

I hesitated. I'd already confessed too much since we'd reconnected months ago. "No…"

"No?" he repeated. He sounded surprised, disappointed, maybe a little hurt.

"No. No. I love you. I fucking *love* you."

He smiled. I went on in a rush. "I spent so many years convincing myself my feelings for you were just a silly schoolboy's dream. I didn't really know you, after all. Well, now I've gotten to know you, and you are exactly who I thought you were. Everything I imagined and loved about you actually exists." I stopped abruptly, embarrassed by yet another unintended confession.

"You really were in love with me back then?"

"I was. *Everyone* was in love with you," I said. "You weren't just on the basketball team, you were the star player! You were in the band. You played the lead in every school play starting with the seventh grade—"

"Yeah, yeah," he said dismissively. "Everyone was in love with the star, the hottest guy in school, but now I'm sure you were the only one who loved *me*."

When I said nothing, he said, "I wish I'd known enough back then to love you back."

"It doesn't matter," I said. "As long as you love me now."

"I do," he said, reaching for his drink.

So, I guess I shouldn't have been surprised when after we'd bade each other a drunken goodnight, he walked into my bedroom and asked, "May I join you?"

When I nodded, he slid in bed next to me and, lying on his back staring at the ceiling, his hands crossed on his chest, said, "I have a confession to make."

I propped myself up on my elbow and looked at him.

"I've been trying to tamp down my feelings for you for months. My love for you, my attraction to you feels so foreign to me. Yet it exists, and I can't deny it anymore. I went to Spain hoping to get some perspective. I thought putting distance between us would extinguish my feelings for you. It didn't. If I'm honest, I was miserable the whole time I was there. I missed you so much.

"Hush," I said. "Stop talking, stop thinking, and just feel…"

I felt his lips on mine and then he was inside me. He entered me again this morning. In between, I got to taste his come, which is thick and sweet as corn syrup.

As he slid inside me for the first time, I thought I might expire from sheer ecstasy. Now, I love being fucked in general, but this was next level. Maybe it was because I'd dreamed of just this for so many years in high school. Maybe it was because it has been so long since I've had sex. Or maybe it was because it was he; because it was I.

He wanted to have breakfast on the deck off the kitchen, so we did. Eggs Benedict, bacon, and mimosas. He was really quiet.

"Are you OK?" I asked, worried he already regretted last night and this morning.

"I'm fine," he said, digging into his eggs. "Why?"

"You seem pensive. I thought you might be regretting…what happened between us."

"You serious? I loved being inside you. The sex was pretty hot— even better than I imagined."

"But? Pun intended," I said nervously.

"I was just thinking that none of the women I've been with would believe this—or understand it."

"What would you tell them?"

He put down his fork, took a swig from his glass, and said, "I'd tell them it was only because it was he; because it was I."

"*Parce que c'était lui; parce que c'était moi.*"

"Huh?" he said.

"You just quoted Michel de Montaigne. I just repeated it in the original French."

"Mr. Fabricant would be thrilled."

"Indeed."

Wednesday, May 30, 2018, St. Jude—"Rio all settled in?" MJ asked.

"I guess," I said, looking around the room and realizing there was no evidence of his presence—except for the two coffee mugs in the sink and the bag of Cafe Bustelo in its distinctive yellow, red, and black packaging.

"How's it going?"

How could I tell her it's been three weeks and we are both nearing sixty but are as horny for each other as teenagers?

"Fine," I said. "Getting to know each other and catching up on what we missed over the years."

"How long is he staying?"

"I've no idea. He doesn't seem to plan much in advance. He doesn't seem to own much either. Just some clothes, his music equipment, and his car—"

"That hooptie in the car port?"

I nodded.

"Good for him," MJ said. "Remember how, back in college, we all swore we wouldn't be tied to possessions like our parents? We would just have books and clothes and maybe a nice stereo?"

"Not me," I said. "I wanted things. I grew up with nothing, so accumulating stuff was always important to me."

Thursday, June 7, 2018, St. Jude—I woke up from a dream about Jackson this morning. Unusually, Rio was still in bed beside me, snoring lightly. I dream of Jackson more often than I like to admit even to myself. I'll open my eyes suddenly in the dark, waking from a dream of him, erect and slightly nauseous, my mouth filled with the taste of barbecue enflamed by too much lighter fluid. The dreams are always searing, *hot*, like sex with Rio. I'll whisper to myself, "I love you, Jackson," even as I snuggle up to a still-sleeping Rio. I know it's insane. I still love Jackson. I love Rio, too. But differently. I don't know him. Still, I hope he knows that despite what happened and whatever comes next, I will always love him. We grew up with so little love that I hope he never feels unloved again.

Tuesday, June 12, 2018, St. Jude—"What was your relationship like?" Rio asked me. We were sitting on the back patio, having drinks and watching the ducks play in the canal.

"With Jackson, you mean?"

He nodded.

"I don't know. I never thought about it. We just were, you know?"

He kept his eyes on me, and I felt the need to keep talking to try to explain, though whether I was explaining to him or myself, I don't know.

"The few guys in my life—you, Juan—were like pieces of the puzzle of me."

"Juan was the guy from the orchard, right?"

"Yeah. Anyway, with Juan, I learned a little more about myself. But when Jackson came along, he fell into my life like the final missing puzzle piece. With him, I got to see the first complete picture of myself, of my life." I paused, shook my head. "Does that make *any* sense at all?" I asked.

"Yeah, it does." He paused. "Can I ask you another question?"

"Of course."

"So where do I fit into this puzzle of yours?"

"Honestly, I don't know. You're the puzzle piece I didn't even know was missing."

We went back to studying the ducks in companionable silence.

Saturday, October 6, 2018, St. Jude—"So what's up with Rio?" MJ asked me.

"What do you mean?"

"It's been six months."

"So?"

"So, are you in love with him?"

"I don't know. Maybe. I don't know. I know I really, really like him. I think he's sexy as hell. Sometimes I think, if I can't be with Jackson, it doesn't really matter who I'm with as long as he's nice. You know?"

She just shook her head. She is as baffled by our affair as I am.

Maybe I'd been seduced by Rio's near-constant declarations of love. Until him, only Jackson had told me he loved me. He'd rarely said the words, but love was in his eyes when he looked at me, was in his touch when he held me, was piled high on the plate of coq au vin he made for dinner on a winter's night, was stacked between the ice cubes in the negroni he'd meet me at the door with every night after work.

"Do you think, it's just because he needs a place to stay?"

I looked at her in surprise.

She blushed slightly. "Sorry. I'm just worried that he might be using you—"

"Everybody uses everybody, don't they?"

MJ laughed, and the moment passed. "Oh, no, Miss Thing, you did *not* just quote Tony Manero to me."

The truth is I don't feel used by Rio, any more than I feel I'm using him. My hunger to feel him inside me is genuine, but it's more than just lust, for he is the little Dutch boy, and I am the leaky dike; his cock, the boy's finger plugging up the hole in me, causing my waters to rise and teem again with life. And with each orgasm he pulls from me, I feel as if I've won a pair of silver skates.

Maybe loving me has enabled Rio to express a side of himself he hadn't been comfortable with before. I worry that he will tire of this adventure and go back to loving women, withdrawing his cock and causing my waters and the life they sustain to ebb away. Again.

"So…back to Rio," MJ said, pulling me out of my thoughts.

"What about him?"

"*Is* he gay?"

I shrugged. "He says he's not. He insists I'm the only man he's ever been attracted to."

"So, he's like only gay for you?"

I shrugged. "I guess…"

"But what do you think?"

"It doesn't matter what I think. I can't decide his orientation for him.

"I still don't get it."

"It's not as unheard of as you may think. There's even a trope in gay romance—mostly written by women for other women— known as 'gay for you only.' It's quite controversial. A lot of people don't believe such a thing exists. Like a lot of people claim bisexuality isn't real."

"But that's just it. Rio isn't even claiming he's bisexual."

"No. I actually don't think he is. Bisexual, I mean. Orientation is simply a pattern of attraction. His attraction has only been to women. For whatever reason, that pattern broke when we reconnected and got to know each other."

In truth, neither Rio nor I can explain his attraction to me. The closest way to explain it, I think, is still as Michel de Montaigne wrote: "Because it was he; because it was I."

MJ sighed. "I suppose I'll never understand any of this."

"What?"

"Romance, being in love, sex."

Rio walked into the room and the conversation ended.

Saturday, December 15, 2018, St. Jude—"O?" Jackson said, unsure.

"Jackson," I said, startled. He was the last person I expected to run into at the mall.

"How have you been, O?"

"OK," I said, not trusting my voice.

The little boy standing beside him tugged at Jackson's pant leg. "Who's he?" he asked, glancing at me.

"He's my friend, Oren. I knew him before you were born."

The little boy looked perplexed, as children do at the concept of a parent having a life before they were born, that there was even existence before them. "Hello," he said to me. "We have the same name."

"We do?"

"This is my son," Jackson said. "His name is Oren."

Surprised, I shot him a questioning look.

"I insisted," he said.

I cocked my head, studying him for a moment.

"It means 'laurel,' which symbolizes the resurrection of Christ."

"Still the preacher's kid."

He smiled.

"How's Kitt?" I asked.

"Kitt is Kitt. She moved to Vancouver. Took Frankenstein and left."

"I'm sorry?" I said. It sounded like a question. Perhaps it was. I wasn't sure I'd heard him right, or more correctly what he'd meant.

"No, you're not. And you don't have to be. I have Oren."

I turned my attention to young Oren, squatting so we were eye to eye. He was a beautiful boy; he looked like his father, I realized. "Nice to meet you, Oren."

Looking up at Jackson, I asked, "How long had it been going on—your affair with Kitt, I mean?"

He glanced at little Oren. "It wasn't an affair. It was one time. Once. She got pregnant."

I saw Rio pulling up behind us. He insists on parking at the farthest corner of every parking lot. I hate that, so he always drops me off first and then goes to get the car and picks me up after. Oren looked at us curiously, and I saw a different ending to our story. "My ride's here," I said, standing up.

Rio leaned out the car window and called out, "Hey, babe, your chariot awaits."

"Is that...*Rio*?" Jackson asked.

"Yes," I said. "I had to learn to live without you."

"I had to learn to live without you too, you know."

I felt my long-simmering anger rising to the surface. "*I* didn't throw us away. *You* did."

"She threatened to have an abortion if I didn't leave you. I couldn't live with that…"

Suddenly I saw Jackson as I had before, once again sixteen years old, this time doing the "right" thing, the *expected* thing.

"Poor Jackson, still my *preacher's kid*," I said more sharply than I'd intended.

"Look, if I had refused, she would have had the abortion and told you anyway, which would have destroyed us. I chose the option with the least collateral damage."

"I have to go," I said and turned to walk away. Seeing me approach the car, Rio swung open his door, hopped out, and with more vigor than I've seen to date outside of sex, and despite his bad hip, he raced around the car to open the passenger door for me. This wasn't unusual; he often opens doors and carries packages for me, but the baleful look he shot Jackson was. Jackson, for his part, glared at Rio.

As Rio and I pulled away from the curb, Jackson knelt behind his son and wrapped his arms around him as they both waved goodbye. Jackson's love for Oren was palpable, even from the distance of the car. I marveled at that, given Jackson was a son unloved, *despised* by his own father, yet he was able to love and cherish his own son.

I went back to thinking about Rio's odd behavior. MJ had recently observed, "Jackson was always a gentleman, and that he cared for you was obvious, but he still treated you like a man. Rio treats like you're his girlfriend." This makes sense to me; Rio is straight, so he has only his relationships with women as a blueprint for our relationship, ergo if he is the man, I have to be by default the "woman." But the possessiveness he'd just displayed couldn't be traced to his understanding of the gender binary. Was he, I wondered suddenly, actually *jealous*?

"He still looks like a thug," Rio said, breaking into my thoughts.

"Jackson? Maybe… There's nothing of the thug in him, though. Never has been. He's a gentleman."

"Unlike me?" Rio shot back sharply.

"You? There's nothing gentle about you. You're a sexy beast." And he is. If Jackson had been my preacher's kid, Rio is my bad boy.

We fell silent. Rio seemed to be thinking hard about something.

"You're awfully quiet," he said, breaking the silence.

"Just thinking," I said. Seeing Jackson had been like rereading an old favorite book—it's not quite as you remembered it, and there are some favorite parts you've forgotten and still others you remember and still love. "He named his son Oren," I added.

"Do you think that means anything in particular?" Rio asked in his usually incisive way.

My mind flashed back to the first terrible days after Jackson's betrayal. I'd demanded to know what happened. He'd shrugged in frustration and said, "I love you. But now I have to love someone else." In my hurt and confusion, I'd assumed he'd meant Kitt, but what if he'd meant Oren, his unborn son, the child he couldn't bear to have aborted? Would that change anything?

"No idea," I said, effectively ending the conversation but continuing to think over everything Jackson had said in our brief conversation.

Rio squeezed my shoulder. "Hey, babe, we're home."

I started.

"Where were you?" he asked. "You seemed so far away."

I just shrugged, but in truth, Jackson had left me with a puzzle. When he'd raised his left hand in goodbye, I'd noticed he still had his wedding ring on. The one I'd given him. And I was puzzled by the odd possessiveness Rio had shown in front of Jackson. As for Jackson, well, I was puzzled by...*everything*. As I got out of the car, I wondered if it was my fate to be perpetually confused by the men in my life.

GRAY (2019)

Monday, January 7, 2019, St. Jude—This morning, we were in the kitchen when one of Rio's songs—a salsa-infused pop song of the sort popular at weddings and bar mitzvahs—came on the radio. "It's your song," I shouted.

He grinned. "Come," I said grabbing his hand, "dance with me."

He pulled away. "No. I've never danced with a man."

"It's no different to dancing with a woman."

I suddenly remembered the time we were at a house party with MJ, and I hurt her feelings by refusing to dance with her because I didn't want anyone to think I was straight.

"Dance with me," I said, "and you can cross one more thing off your 'never have I ever' bucket list.

"Can you even salsa?"

"I sure can. Jackson and I took ballroom dancing classes for years. We danced competitively, too. Won a few. Lost more." I laughed, remembering the days without bitterness.

"Speaking of Jackson…"

"Yes?" He seldom brought Jackson up.

"You told me once that when he betrayed you, he broke your heart, that'd he left behind only a small piece of your heart for living and breathing."

"It was true," I said quietly. "That's how I felt."

"But even with that little piece of your heart with just enough room for living and breathing, you've made me feel more loved these last few months than I have in my entire life."

Friday, October 11, 2019, St. Jude—Today is my birthday. MJ video-called this morning to sing me happy birthday as she always does.

"Thanks, hon," I said.

"So, any big plans for today?" She and I and Rio are going out to dinner to celebrate tomorrow because she is off on weekends.

"No. Yesterday, Rio took me on a cheese-and-wine train ride to celebrate. The train stopped in a town literally named Paradise before starting the return leg of the trip."

"How was it?"

"It was great. We were seated in soft, upholstered captain's chairs that swiveled so we could take in the countryside as it sauntered past. Built in 1911, the parlor car in which we—and a handful of other couples—were seated was resplendent with late-Victorian elegance."

"That sounds awfully romantic," MJ said.

"I suppose it was." And it had been, until we stopped in Paradise and our waiter came over with a new wine for us to sample and remarked, "Y'all are so cute." I guess we were. Rio had attempted to tame his wild curls with little success. Between his wild mane of hair and his rumpled, slightly snug wool blazer and plaid scarf, he looked charmingly eccentric. I, according to MJ, with my small frame, stellar wardrobe, and poised confidence, look like an undernourished former model.

"I hope me and my boyfriend are still together when we're your age," he continued brightly as he poured wine. "How long have y'all been together?"

"We're not...together," Rio said.

"Oh," our waiter said, just as another passenger called out to him, allowing him to skip away from his embarrassment. I stared into the distance over Rio's shoulder.

"Sorry," he said suddenly. "I really blew that, didn't I?"

I looked at him but said nothing.

"I'm sorry," he said again. "In my head, we're together. But it never occurred to me that other people would look at us and see that we're together."

"Wow," MJ said when I related the story to her. "How can you have a romance with someone who is straight? Rio *is* straight, isn't he?"

I shrugged. *Who needs labels?* I wondered. Labels are neat, orderly, convenient, but life, love, *attraction* is messy, disorderly, so what is the point of assigning labels to any of it?

I sighed. "Rio is...actually, I don't know what Rio is...or what being in a relationship with me makes him. I'm not sure he does either. I'm not sure it even matters."

"Let me ask you this: are you happy?"

"I am," I said, "but I'm frustrated too."

"Why?"

"Rio doesn't *do* anything. He says he wants to write this children's book—"

"Why does everyone think they can write a children's book?"

"I know, right? Still, at least it would give him something to do. I bought him a new laptop, thinking that would help because the one he has is so crappy. I seem to make all the decisions for us—"

"Well, in all fairness, you did that with Jackson, too."

"Oh, I suppose I did. I wonder why?"

"Because you're a bossy bottom."

I looked at her in surprise.

"Oh, don't look so surprised," she said. "I have other gay friends. I hear…things…"

"Point taken. Wait, what makes you think I'm a bottom?"

"Oren, that cannot be a serious question."

With a chuckle, I said, "OK, I'll concede that point as well."

"OK. Next question. Do you love him?"

"Maybe."

"But not like you loved Jackson?"

MJ knows me so well. Still, I was curious. "Why do you say that?"

"I've been around you and Jackson, and I've been around you and Rio…"

"And?" I prompted.

"Rio seems…enchanted by you. He exudes desire, an urge to merge with you, get under your skin even. Jackson wanted only to love and care for you. You wanted to succeed so you could give Jackson the world. I see a little of that with Rio—you seem to want to shelter him while at the same time surrendering yourself to him. And that's fine. It seems to make your relationship work."

"You're right," I said. "I suppose I don't love Rio like I loved Jackson. But see, here's the thing, all our lives together, I could never imagine myself with anyone *but* Jackson."

"And now?"

"Now, I know the only *other* person I could be with is Rio."

"Why?"

"Because he's Rio. Because I like who I am when I'm with him. Because he feels the same way."

Saturday, October 19, 2019, St. Jude—Rio pulled back and his weight eased off me as he lowered my legs from his shoulders. Sex with him is always intense. But tonight, there was a kind of desperation in the way he made love to me—like he was searching for something he feared he'd lost. I thought about what MJ had said about him wanting to get under my skin. He flopped onto his back. I leaned over and kissed his nipple. "I'm gonna go hop in the shower," I said.

When I returned to the bedroom, Rio was turned on his side, his back to my side of the bed. I spilled into bed, and inhaling his scent, I curled around him and kissed his back. He pulled away. "Something wrong? I asked, startled. He rolled onto his back and stared up at the ceiling.

"I love our connection. I love *you*. I'm happy. In this house. Here. With. You—"

"But—"

"But what?"

"I don't know, but I sensed a but coming." He struggled to sit up and I knew his hip was hurting. I cleared my throat. "Are you still upset about that waiter?"

"He labeled us a couple," he blurted.

"He did. *I* didn't. I've never asked you to label us…or yourself."

"The fact is that we *are* a couple. And no matter how often I say I'm with you because you're you and I'm me—the fact of the matter is I am in love with a man."

I remained silent, whether from the shock of his admission or the depth of his unhappiness, I did not know. Watching me, he sighed and said, "I'm sorry. When I started this affair with you, I was curious. I thought it was a phase, a new adventure…"

"And now?"

"Now this—us—*you*—is starting to feel like habit."

"Oh," I said.

"Listen," he said, crushing me, "I'm gonna go sleep in the other room. OK?"

"OK," I said and watched him, naked, walk away.

Friday, October 25, 2019, St. Jude—When I woke up this morning, Rio wasn't in bed beside me. This wasn't unusual. Often when his hip is particularly painful, he'll get up and go sleep in the guest room, and it had been rainy and damp yesterday, which always makes his hip hurt.

The guest room was empty, and the dresser drawers were partially open, the closet door ajar. I set about straightening the room—his messiness and inability to complete tasks frustrates me. As it was early in the morning and I was still half-asleep, I just slammed the drawers shut and closed the closet door without realizing they were empty of his clothes.

In the kitchen, there was freshly brewed coffee—Rio, like Jackson, held the secret to making great fresh coffee. After pouring a cup, I wandered through the open front door to find Rio loading his things into his ancient Subaru. Its bright-yellow color seemed faded, and its red-and-black pinstripe was flaking off in places.

"Morning," he called, seeing me, but not pausing in his efforts.

"Morning," I repeated, then asked, "What's going on?"

"It's time for me to move on," he said. He turned to face me, his hand shielding his eyes from the sunlight.

"Oh," I said. "Oh. OK." And just like that, our—*whatever this was*—ended. I can't say I wasn't hurt, even though I hadn't expected anything else, hadn't been able to quantify our relationship or define what I wanted from him. Still, like Peter Lawford in *Sweet November*, I wanted to postpone this parting; I wanted to add days to the calendar to prolong our togetherness, to give us time we did not have and which perhaps I did not deserve. In the end, I did not throw myself at his feet and beg him not to leave, beg him not to be another man I loved leaving me behind in the dust. I did not attempt to alter the calendar to trick him into believing our time together hadn't come to an end.

Instead, I simply went back into the house and sat on the deck of the kitchen from where I could hear him humming as he finished loading his car, then the sound of his car sliding down the gravel driveway. I was reminded of Sidney Poitier's character singing "Amen" while packing his wagon and slipping away at the end of *Lilies of the Field*. I suppose, like Sidney's character, Rio felt that having rebuilt the chapel of me that Kitt had burned to the ground, it was simply time for him to move on.

I stood and watched for his car as it backed down the driveway. I'd always been frustrated by his unwillingness—his inability—to finish anything he started. But he had finished something at last; he'd finished us. I watched until his car, smoking, eased off the gravel drive onto the road and disappeared.

I'll miss Rio, but I'll survive. Hell, if I survived losing Jackson, I'd surely survive this parting. Rio was a blip on my radar, a passing diversion, and I'd known he was a bit of a nomad.

Saturday, November 16, 2019, St. Jude—MJ is the most popular anchorwoman in our city in a generation. Thus, when out in public, she is often besieged by adoring fans, just asking if she is really Mary Jane Mitchell; others ask for autographs; and still others, more intrusive, ask her to pose for selfies with them. This happens at Saks, at Nordstrom, at restaurants, even while standing on a corner waiting to cross the street. Once while standing in a disorganized line at the post office, several people, recognizing her, implored her to do an exposé of the inefficiency and general incompetence of staff at the local post office.

So, I wasn't surprised today at lunch when our drinks were interrupted by a young woman who approached and asked to take a selfie with her while her boyfriend stood nearby looking embarrassed. After the selfie, the young woman turned to me and, eyeing me up and down, asked, "Should I take a selfie with you, too?"

"I beg your pardon?" I asked.

She sighed with dramatic exasperation. "Should I take a selfie with you?" she repeated. "Are you anybody? You look like you could be somebody," she added, taking in my dangling double-cross earrings, goatee, and open wing-collared tuxedo shirt.

Before I could answer, "No," MJ snapped, "He's my friend. He is everybody."

Suitably chastised, the young woman nodded and walked away but not before I heard her say to her companion, "I should have known he was nobody. I didn't recognize him."

In a rare moment of fury, MJ started to rise to her feet. My hand on the sleeve of her vintage pink Chanel bouclé suit—MJ is also the best-dressed anchorwoman on TV—arrested her movement.

She settled in her seat. "How are you doing?" she asked, laying her hand over mine and entwining our fingers, "since Rio left? The coward."

I casually disengaged our fingers—I am always uncomfortable with displays of physical affection with female friends in public. It makes me feel deceptive somehow, as if I am sending a dishonest message, a misdirection.

"I'm fine," I said. "I survived losing both my parents *and* Jackson. This is *nothing*—"

"This isn't nothing," she said carefully while scanning the menu in front of her.

"No. I suppose not. Still—"

"You're not gonna say your affair with Rio was a bad idea? It wasn't—"

"No. It wasn't. But it wasn't a particularly good idea, either."

"How do you mean?" she asked, putting down her menu.

"I know I was in love with him on some level. Certainly, there was something thrilling about getting a chance at love with my teenage crush. And yeah, he was in love with me too. But sometimes I'd wonder what he was playing at. He often seemed uncomfortable with our relationship—he told me he worried that I was becoming a habit, whatever that means. At other times, he seemed impatient, like he was stuck in bed waiting for a stubborn fever to pass so he could get back to living his life."

"I think that's bitterness talking," MJ said. "You were together a year and a half. I saw you two together. I didn't understand it, but straight or not, he was definitely in love with you."

"That's part of Rio's charm—making you believe his nonsense. He convinced me that our romance was special, that he was only able to love me, a man, because I was I and he was he."

"You don't think that's true anymore?"

I shrugged.

"Well, let me tell you this," MJ said. "When you and he were together, you looked happier than I've seen you at any point since Jackson left."

"I guess I just feel really stupid. I really did—do—love Rio. And I thought—improbable as it was—that he loved me. It never occurred to me that he would just walk away one day."

"I get that."

"Why does everyone find it so easy to leave me?"

"Who's everyone?"

"Grampy Eddie, Dad, Mom, Juan, Jackson, Rio…"

"Rio was an asshole. He dropped you like a bad habit. But Grampy Eddie and your parents didn't choose to leave you—they *died*. Juan was a picking-season romance and you were fifteen. And I know Jackson didn't find it easy to leave you."

My head snapped up and my tears stopped. "Thank you for canceling my pity party. You're right. I'm being a jerk."

"You're human. You're hurt. Give yourself the grace to grieve." She covered my hand with hers; I fought the urge to pull away.

"Let's order lunch," I said, "and speak of other things."

MJ nodded and picked up her menu again while signaling the waiter to bring another round of drinks. She knew our conversation had gone as far as it could because I don't do vulnerable.

"How's *your* love life these days?" I asked to make up for my shortcoming. "Tell me."

"There's nothing to tell."

"Why don't you ever talk about it?"

"Oren, there is literally nothing to tell. I don't have a love life."

"Oh. Well, now that I've sworn off men, I can help you find one. Let's see… You're beautiful, you've been voted best dressed TV personality how many times? You're famous—"

"Stop," she said, throwing her hands up in surrender. "I don't actually want a man."

"Oh—"

"I mean men are fine, though gay ones are less irritating—"

"True, that."

"I've had affairs. They all ended in tears—*theirs* by the way, not mine. It eventually dawned on me that I didn't really want to be in a romantic relationship. And I don't like sex—"

"You don't like sex?"

"No, it's too...*intimate.* It always leaves me feeling as if I've been cut open for some man to gaze at my innards. And it's messy. And you know how I hate messy. I can't even have kids, so I finally asked myself what was the point of enduring something I don't enjoy? Oh, and kissing, well, that's just gross."

I stared at her in stupefaction. How had we been friends this long and I did not know this about her?

"Have I shocked you?" she asked.

"No, no. I'm just surprised you never said anything before.

She shrugged. "I don't think about it much. I have a great life, the career I dreamed of, friends like you."

"I'd like to propose a toast," I said. "To you—for knowing what you want and don't and for living your best life accordingly."

We clinked glasses. "By the way," she said, "I think Perils is seeing Toderick again."

I rolled my eyes. "They'd better elope this time," I said. "I'm not buying them a third wedding present."

"And I'm not buying a third bridesmaid dress or planning another shower."

"Amen," I added, and we clinked glasses again.

Monday, December 9, 2019, St. Jude—I ran into Jackson unexpectedly again at the mall today. I was wandering aimlessly when I heard, "Oren?"

I wheeled around. "Jackson!"

I stared at him. He was dressed all in gray: gray jeans tucked into gray-and-black Doc Martens, and a dove-gray cable-knit turtleneck under a pebble-gray sheepskin bomber jacket lined with shearling. I was startled because it wasn't anything from our shared wardrobe. In all our years together, Jackson had never shopped for clothes; he'd simply worn whatever I bought for myself.

"We have to stop meeting like this," he joked.

"What are you doing here?" I asked.

"Claude took Oren to see *The Nutcracker*, so I thought I'd do some Christmas shopping. Oren was so excited. He said Claude told him it was a 'date' so it had to be just the two of them, so Octavio wasn't allowed to go."

"I'm glad you stayed close with them."

"They have been a godsend, especially after Kitt first left. There I was with an infant I had no idea how to take care of."

I nodded.

"So, what are you doing? Christmas shopping?"

"No. I don't really have anyone to shop for. I really just like looking at all the gifts for sale and feeling the excitement of the shoppers and imagining their collective delight when they exchange and open perfectly wrapped gifts…I'm sorry, that sounds pitiful, doesn't it."

"No," Jackson said. "It sounds like you."

I nodded.

"How's Rio?" he asked me suddenly.

I shrugged. "Fine, I guess. He moved to Italy, where he appears to be growing his hair and roses beside a woman named Poppy."

"Oh!" he said. "I'm sorry. I know he was your *it* boy."

"He was," I said. "But *you* were the love of my life." And with that admission, I let go of Rio fully and once and for all.

He looked at me sharply, clearly startled. For my part, I was embarrassed to have admitted so much when I didn't intend to. Hoping to change the subject, I asked, "How about you? Are you seeing anyone?"

"No," he said. "There have been a few guys, mostly younger. It's hard when you bring a kid into the mix. None of them stuck. None of them were you." Now it was his turn to look embarrassed. "The truth is," he continued in a rush, "I don't know who I am without you. I don't know how to *be* without you."

And there we were, two halves of the same tree, each leaning against air.

Jackson broke the awkward silence. "I'm actually glad I ran into you," he said. "You've been on my mind a lot lately."

"Why?"

"I never apologized to you—for hurting you, for destroying us. I'm truly sorry. You deserved better. I would never in a million years have thought I'd be the one to hurt you. In my clumsy attempt to lessen your pain, I implied that I'd stopped loving you—I hadn't—haven't—"

He looked so distraught, so much like the old Jackson, *my* Jackson, my PK, my preacher's kid, I wanted to take him in my arms and comfort him. Instead, I asked, "How's little Oren?"

Jackson beamed. "He's good. He's in preschool. Growing like a weed. Smart as a whip. Always has his nose in a book—he reminds me of you…"

"Face it, you're a bookworm magnet."

Jackson laughed, a warm familiar sound I hadn't heard in ages and hadn't realized until now, I'd missed.

"And co-parenting with Kitt is working out OK?"

"No. Last month, I filed for and got full custody of Oren after years of no contact—no calls or texts—not even a card on his birthday—from Kitt."

"I'm sorry. Why—"

"She thought she could replace you," he said quietly.

I glanced at his left hand, at the platinum wedding band I'd first placed on his finger at the jewelry counter in Tiffany so long ago. He followed my eyes, twisted his ring with his left hand self-consciously. "I couldn't bring myself to take it off. That would have felt like I'd lost you completely. Do you mind?"

Afraid to speak, I shook my head no in response to his question. Looking at him, watching his face, seeing the way he looked at me, I wondered if we could find love again on the other side of the apocalypse. If we could, it was only *because it was he; because it was I.*

"Why are you wearing two watches?" he asked.

"Because wearing one would have felt like losing you completely."

He looked at me, puzzled. *Shut up, you ass*, I told myself, *before you make this conversation more awkward.* Then, before I could stop myself, I blurted, "Do you want to get lunch?"

EPILOGUE

Oren woke up, as he often did, because he needed to pee. Once awake, he discovered little Oren had crawled into bed between them. He and Jackson curled towards him like protecting brackets; his and Jackson's fingers entwined across the boy's narrow waist.

A slight breeze sent the fragrance of night-blooming jasmine in through the open windows; the scent covered the three of them like a favorite old blanket. Oren raised his hand up as if to catch the breeze. He lowered his hand back down and fought the urge to pee, hoping to settle back into sleep. *Here we are,* he thought, lying in the dark. *This is where we belong.* In this place they unexpectedly found themselves, there was laughter and love and a rather plodding domesticity. Claude had been right; their love for each other hadn't been destroyed. It had merely gone into hiding like the sun at dusk waiting for a new day when it would reclaim its place in the firmament and shine once again.

It occurred to him that this was it, that *this was everything,* and realizing he would not change anything about their lives, that he couldn't wish for more, Oren drifted into sleep. Just before he fell fully asleep, he thought: *I must call Claude.*

ACKNOWLEDGEMENTS

Writing is a lonely profession, and my life would be much lonelier and less colorful without these folks. In no particular order, I'd like to thank:

My publishing family at Beaten Track Publishing for always believing in me, supporting and nurturing me and my talent.

Denisse Nichols for helping me navigate the writing landscape and find my footing.

Lily Harper and the team at Go Edge Creative for their guidance, flexibility, and marketing expertise.

My friend, neighbor, and fellow author, Kathy Anderson—our regular meetups at Billy Murphy's to discuss the writer's life and celebrate our successes mean the world to me.

And finally, my husband Stanley—I love you for always encouraging me to follow my dreams.

ABOUT THE AUTHOR

Bronx-born wordsmith, Larry Benjamin considers himself less a writer than an artist whose chosen medium is the written word rather than clay or paint or bronze. He is the author of the gay novels *Excellent Sons: A Love Story in Three Acts* (2022 Lambda Literary Award winner in the Gay Romance category and a 2022 Next Generation Indie Book Award Finalist), *Unbroken* (2014 Lambda Literary Award finalist and a 2014 IPPY—Independent Publishers Book Award—Gold medalist), *The Sun, the Earth & the Moon,* and *In His Eyes*. He is also the author the allegorical novella *Vampire Rising*.

He lives in Philadelphia with his husband and two rescue dogs named Atticus and Gatsby.

Website: www.larrybenjamin.com

BY THE AUTHOR

Unbroken

Vampire Rising

The Christmas Present

Black & Ugly

In His Eyes

The Sun, the Earth & the Moon

Excellent Sons: A Love Story in Three Acts

He

beatentrackpublishing.com/larrybenjamin

www.ingramcontent.com/pod-product-compliance
Lightning Source LLC
Chambersburg PA
CBHW012150260626
47155CB00020B/3548